DOCTOR WHO
PLANET OF EVIL

THE CHANGING FACE OF DOCTOR WHO
The cover illustration of this book portrays
the fourth DOCTOR WHO

DOCTOR WHO AND THE PLANET OF EVIL

Based on the BBC television serial *The Planet of Evil* by Louis Marks by arrangement with the British Broadcasting Corporation

TERRANCE DICKS

A TARGET BOOK
published by
The Paperback Division of
W. H. Allen & Co. Ltd

A Target Book
Published in 1977
by the Paperback Division of W. H. Allen & Co. Ltd
A Howard & Wyndham Company
123 King Street, London W6 9JG

Published simultaneously in Great Britain by
Allan Wingate (Publishers) Ltd, 1977

Printed in Great Britain by
Richard Clay (The Chaucer Press) Ltd., Bungay, Suffolk

ISBN 0 426 11682 8

Contents

Killer Planet

The planet was alive.

Not just with the life that swarmed in the teeming jungles. There was another kind of life, something ancient, alien, hostile to man. It was as if the entire planet was one colossal living being that watched, waited, chose its moment and *struck*.

Eight men had come to explore this remote planet on the fringes of the known universe. A survey team from the mighty Morestran Empire, equipped with all the technology of a super-civilisation. Eight men had landed—now there were three.

The planet was alive—and it was a killer.

The prefabricated plastic survival dome nestled incongruously in the jungle clearing. The 'instant house' of the space-age, the dome provided both laboratory and shelter for the survey team. Five of the team now had no further need of the dome. Their graves were in a row just in front of it. The fifth grave was freshly dug.

Braun, one of the three survivors, was at work on this latest grave. He patted the earth into a smooth mound with a trowel and thrust a metal identity plaque into the soil. The plaque read:

Edgar Lumb
Morestran Pioneer
Died here 7y2 in the year 37,166

Braun thought about gathering some jungle flowers for the grave, then shook his head wearily. The flowers were part of the planet—and the planet had killed Lumb, and all the others. He looked up at the sky. Daylight on this planet was little more than a blue haze at best, and the haze was darkening now. Braun took out his sextant and took a reading on the distant sun that glowed feebly, a thousand light-years away. The reading confirmed his fears. It would be night soon—and night was the dangerous time. He must warn the others.

Braun went back inside the dome, moved over to the communications set, and began to call.

Not far from the dome, the jungle thinned out into a rocky plain, beyond which lay the lower slopes of some far-distant mountains. At the very edge of the jungle was a place the survey team had christened the Black Pool. The reasons for the name were obvious enough—it was a pool, and it was most certainly black. No ordinary blackness, but a dense *total* blackness that seemed to defeat the eye. There was never a ripple on the surface of the pool, and it refused to reflect light, or anything else. The explorers didn't

8

even know what the pool was composed of—it could have been water, oil or some totally alien substance. Since their purposes were mainly geological, they left the pool strictly alone.

It was the rocky area around the pool which interested them. Its reddish-coloured rocks had proved amazingly rich in mineral deposits, and the geologists spent a great deal of time there. Two of them, two out of the surviving three, were at work there now.

Baldwin, a thin nervous man, was using a hand power-drill to extract rock samples from varying depths below the surface, methodically transferring the samples to thick-walled protective canisters. He passed each filled canister across to Professor Sorenson, head of the expedition, who examined the contents with a stereometer, set up on a portable work bench.

Both men were tired and tense, with red-rimmed eyes and stubbled cheeks. Their space coveralls were grimy and dishevelled, torn by the vicious jungle thorns. Baldwin worked with gloomy determination. Since he was trapped on this hell-planet, there was nothing else to do, and the gradual shrinking in their numbers had cast an impossible work-load on the survivors. Baldwin was almost grateful for the endless work. It stopped him thinking about the fate of the others—about his own fate if the rescue expedition failed to arrive on time.

Professor Sorenson, on the other hand, worked with feverish intensity, like a man racing against time, on the brink of some tremendous discovery. A stocky fair-haired man in his early fifties, Sorenson had been completely transformed by his time on the planet. He had become obsessed, determined to wrench the secrets from a world that seemed equally determined to defeat him. He worked like a machine, transcribing his results into the recorder at his side. The two men worked in silence, both too weary for conversation.

There was a beep from the communicator and Baldwin picked it up.

'Baldwin here.'

Braun's voice crackled over the receiver. 'Base checking. You two O.K.?'

'All quiet.'

'Where are you?'

'Sector five—by the Black Pool. We've hit a rich lode.'

Braun's voice sounded agitated. 'Sector five? Listen, I've just taken a sun shot. You have fifteen degrees till full night. You'd better get out of there fast!'

'Right. On our way.' Baldwin put back the headset and turned to Sorenson, who didn't seem to have registered the interruption. 'That was Braun, Professor. We've got to leave.'

Sorenson looked up abstractedly. 'Leave? Why?'

'Fifteen degrees to full night, that's why.'

Sorenson tapped the canister he was working on. 'Just look at this, Baldwin. It's showing more than seventy per cent pure!'

Patiently Baldwin said, 'Sir, we'll never make base

before dark if we don't leave *now*.'

Sorenson shook his head. 'We can't leave now. The last time we hit a vein as rich as this, you know what happened.'

'Lorenzo died,' said Baldwin bluntly. 'And he was just the first. That's when all the trouble started.'

'Yes, yes, I know.' Sorenson spoke impatiently, as if Lorenzo's death was a very minor matter. 'But you remember what else happened? We lost the lode. The ore-vein vanished. This damned planet took it back!' He glanced round at the edge of the jungle. 'It's alive, you know that, Baldwin? It watches every move we make.'

Baldwin was already packing up his kit. 'Professor, please. We must go.'

'No! I won't be beaten again. I'm staying here till the analysis is finished.'

'There isn't time, Professor. We can come back to-morrow.'

'The vein could have vanished by tomorrow.' Sorenson grabbed Baldwin's arm. 'Don't you understand? The planet *knows*—it senses what we're trying to do!'

Baldwin pulled away. 'Well *I'm* not trekking through that jungle after dark. If you don't come now, I shall have to leave you.'

Sorenson waved a dismissive hand. 'Then leave. Leave!' He returned to his analysis of the samples.

Baldwin picked up his pack, and hesitated for a moment. But Sorenson was already deep in his work. He was totally absorbed and clearly quite beyond reason. The blue haze was much darker now—it would soon be night. Baldwin shouldered his pack and trudged off into the jungle. Sorenson didn't even see him go.

Braun was pacing anxiously about the survival dome, glancing at his wrist-chronometer every few seconds. If the other two had left promptly they should have been back by now. Finally he could bear the suspense no longer. Snatching a blaster-rifle from a wall-rack, he ran out of the dome.

Just as he reached the middle of the clearing something strange and horrible happened. There was a sound—a kind of alien crackling, like a geiger-counter magnified a hundred times. Braun had heard that sound before—and each time it had heralded the death of one of his friends. He turned to run, but something vast, shapeless and invisible flowed over him and *absorbed* him. As the invisible alien entity sucked him in, Braun too became invisible. Slowly he vanished, struggling wildly, cursing and screaming, firing useless bolts from his rifle. Feet, legs, body disappeared. The invisible tide crept higher, swallowing head and shoulders. With a last terrible scream, Braun vanished completely. The alien sound moved on towards the dome.

Not far away, Baldwin was running towards the clearing. It was gloomy enough in the jungle at the best of times, and now, with night fast approaching, it was darker than ever. Strange twisted tree-shapes loomed up at him, tough vines wound themselves round his feet and jagged thorns ripped at his clothing. Baldwin felt the jungle was trying to hold him, trap him. He tore himself free of its grip and staggered on.

It was dark by the time he reached the clearing, and saw the lights of the survival dome. With a sob of relief he crossed the clearing and ran inside. 'Braun!' he yelled, 'Braun, where are you? Sorenson wouldn't come ...' He stopped and looked round in puzzlement. The dome was empty. And the door had been open. If Braun had come to look for them—why hadn't they met on the way?

Suddenly a crackling sound filled the dome. It seemed to come from all around him. Baldwin glared round wildly. He felt some invisible force surrounding him, drawing him in. With a final desperate effort he managed to reach the Space Emergency Alarm on the communications set and press the button. Then the invisible monster swallowed him, and, like Braun, he vanished ...

Through that strange Vortex, where Time and Space are one, sped the incongruous shape of an old blue Police Box, the kind used on the planet Earth in the mid-twentieth century. This particular Police Box was not a Police Box at all, but the Space/Time craft of that mysterious traveller known as the Doctor. It was called the TARDIS, a name made up from the initial letters of 'Time And Relative Dimensions In

Space'. In addition to its many other amazing attributes, the TARDIS was 'dimensionally transcendental'—which simply meant it was bigger on the inside than on the outside.

Inside the TARDIS was a large ultra-modern control room, dominated by the many-sided control console in the centre. Over this console hovered a tall man in comfortable Bohemian-looking clothes. An incredibly long scarf dangled round his neck and a broad-brimmed soft hat was jammed precariously on to a tangle of curly hair. His usually cheerful face was set in a frown of concentration, and his hands were moving a little frantically over the controls.

Watching him with increasing suspicion was a slender dark-haired girl in twentieth-century dress. Her name was Sarah Jane Smith. Back on Earth she was a freelance journalist, but for some time now she had been the Doctor's companion on his journeys in the TARDIS

What was upsetting Sarah was the fact that this particular journey was supposed to be a very short one, at least in inter-galactic terms. In theory the TARDIS was taking them from Loch Ness in the highlands of Scotland, back to UNIT Headquarters near London. The Doctor had been assisting Brigadier Lethbridge-Stewart to deal with the creature that had become known as the Loch Ness Monster, and with its Zygon masters.* When the adventure was over, he had persuaded a rather reluctant Sarah to return with him in the TARDIS, rather than take

* See *Doctor Who and the Loch Ness Monster*.

the train with the Brigadier and his assistant Harry Sullivan.

It was a decision Sarah was beginning to regret. The journey, which should surely have been over in a flash, seemed to have lasted for a very long time. Moreover, the Doctor had been labouring over the console in increasing agitation, while at the same time refusing to answer any of Sarah's questions, or to admit that the somewhat erratic steering mechanism of the TARDIS had once more gone wrong.

Determined to get his attention, Sarah raised her voice. '*How* long have we been travelling, Doctor?'

The Doctor didn't hear—or didn't choose to. 'Mm? What did you say?'

Sarah refused to be put off. 'You promised we'd be back in London five minutes *before* we left Loch Ness.'

The Doctor moved round the console. 'Did I? Did I really say that?'

'You're trying to wriggle out of it,' accused Sarah.

'Wriggle out of what?'

'Out of your promise to take me straight back to London.'

'My dear Sarah, we're travelling through the Space/Time continuum, and you're making a ridiculous fuss about a few minutes!'

Sarah gave a sigh of resignation. 'I see. All right, Doctor, what's gone wrong this time?'

'Wrong? What makes you think anything's gone wrong?' Warning lights began flashing in the far side of the console. The Doctor dashed round and

15

started flicking controls like a supermarket cashier adding up a bill. 'There's *nothing* wrong, Sarah. Nothing at all.'

'Oh yes, there is,' Sarah said firmly. 'You always start being rude when you're trying to cover up a mistake.'

'How well you know me!' The Doctor smiled ruefully. 'Honestly, Sarah, it's nothing very much. Just a slight Time/Space overshoot—easily rectified.'

'Overshoot? What does that mean?'

'Well, if we emerge from the Space/Time vortex *now*, we'll probably come out at the wrong point— a few miles too far, and a few years too late.'

'How many years?'

'Oh, about thirty thousand,' said the Doctor airily.

Sarah winced. 'And how many miles?'

'Difficult to say. Possibly somewhere on the very edge of the Universe . . .'

A bright red light began flashing on the TARDIS console, and an ear-splitting bleep filled the control room. Sarah jumped back, wondering if the TARDIS was about to blow up. 'What's that?'

'A distress signal. Someone's in trouble!'

'Where?'

'Who knows? Stand by for emergency dematerialisation!' The Doctor's hands moved swiftly over the controls.

Emergency dematerialisation was like normal dematerialisation, only noisier and bumpier. When the TARDIS finally juddered to a halt, the Doctor took a quick instrument-reading and opened the doors. He

16

produced a compass-like device from a locker, and dashed out into the night. Sarah shouted, 'Hey, wait for me, Doctor!' and followed him out. There really didn't seem anything else to do.

Outside the TARDIS they paused and looked around. Sarah wasn't in the least surprised to find that they'd arrived in the middle of a particularly sinister-looking alien jungle, at what appeared to be the dead of night. The Doctor closed the TARDIS doors and checked the readings on his direction-finder. He pointed. 'It's that way, Sarah. There seems to be a sort of over-grown track. We'd better hurry —the readings are getting fainter already.' The Doctor started thrusting his way through the jungle.

In the survival dome the beeping of the transmitter became fainter and fainter as the nearly-exhausted batteries ran down.

Deeper in the jungle the Doctor stopped, and looked at the direction-finder. 'It's no good. The signal's gone completely.'

'That's marvellous, Doctor. We don't know what year we're in, we don't know what planet we're on, we're in the middle of a nasty-looking jungle—and now we're lost!'

For a moment they stood and looked at each other. The jungle seemed to be closing in around them.

2

The Probe

The Doctor started casting about in a circle, looking for the faintest flicker on the direction-finder needle. 'With any luck, we're near enough to reach whoever-it-is before whatever-it-was that made them transmit the call overwhelmed them. That is, if we're not too late already.'

Sarah wouldn't be put off. '*Do* you know what planet we're on?'

'Well, it was a weak signal, you see, as if something was muffling it and allowing for the refractive interference of the time warp—aha! There's a trace leading this way. Come on Sarah, can't you walk any faster?'

The Doctor set off again, and Sarah followed, grumbling. 'I'm doing the best I can . . .' Suddenly she stopped, her eyes widening. She stumbled blindly into a tree and clutched it for support.

The Doctor noticed Sarah wasn't with him, turned and ran back to her. 'What's the matter, Sarah? Are you all right?'

Sarah stared blankly at him. 'I think so . . . I don't know. I suddenly felt so . . . *odd* As if my mind was being drawn out of my body . . .'

The Doctor looked hard at her. 'How are you feeling now?'

'Better I think. It seems to be fading ...' Sarah rubbed her eyes and straightened up. 'I'm fine now.'

'I think we'd better get away from here.' The Doctor took Sarah's hand and helped her forward, then stopped as he felt something hard and metallic underfoot. He picked it up and examined it.

'What have you found?'

The Doctor held out the object. It was a cross between an axe and a hammer, made entirely of metal, and badly rusted and corroded. 'A hand tool of some kind.' He thrust it into one of his deep pockets.

Sarah brightened. 'So the people who sent the signal are human—or at least, humanoid.'

The Doctor looked quizzically at her and Sarah said defensively, 'Well at least they've got hands instead of tentacles.' It was all very well for the Doctor to say one life form was just the same as another. He was used to that sort of thing. Sarah felt happier with more human types—it was easier to tell the goodies from the baddies.

The Doctor grinned. 'Come on, Sarah. Human or not, someone still needs our help!' He led the way on through the jungle.

The Morestran Probe Spaceship moved smoothly into orbit around the planet. On the control deck two men studied the instrument screens, which were producing a constant stream of scientific data.

In the command chair sat Controller Salamar; young, fair-haired, very conscious of his rank, a handsome figure in the ornate uniform of the Morestran Space Service. In the number two seat on his left was Vishinsky, a very different figure. Taller, older, with thinning hair and a tough, weary face, Vishinsky was a hardened professional with over thirty years service behind him. Unlike Salamar, who had reached command rank very young, Vishinsky had no highly-placed friends in politics to push forward his promotion. So it was Salamar who sat in the command chair and wore the gold braid. But the Space Service put Vishinsky beside him—just to be sure.

Vishinsky yawned and stretched. 'Well, here we are, Controller ... Zeta Minor. The last planet of the known universe ...'

Salamar frowned, annoyed as always by Vishinsky's casual manner. He leaned forward and spoke into a communications mike. 'This is the Controller. Stabilise orbital position. Ponti and De Haan to Command Deck.' He turned to Vishinsky. 'You will lead the landing party.' Salamar spoke with malicious satisfaction. It would do Vishinsky good to get out of that chair and face some real work.

Vishinsky raised his eyebrows. 'Why not Ponti? He's Executive Officer. And he's younger than I am. Let him be the hero!'

As soon as he'd spoken, Vishinsky knew it was a mistake. Conscious of his own inexperience, Salamar could never take advice or criticism. Question one of his decisions and he invariably turned obstinate.

Sure enough Salamar snapped, 'You are the most experienced officer. *You* will go.'

Vishinsky nodded. 'O.K. But you'll be doing a survey from the ship first?'

'No.'

'Controller, it's advised procedure before landing on any unknown planet.'

Salamar smiled triumphantly. 'Technically, Zeta Minor isn't an unknown planet. Professor Sorenson and his party have been on the surface for several months now.'

'They may also have been dead for several months. We're here because they've not reported back.'

Salamar was getting angry. 'You're aware of our fuel position. Simply getting this far used up most of the Probe's emergency reserve. I cannot waste more fuel on a low-level survey.'

Vishinsky stood up. 'It's your decision, Controller. I'll get equipped for descent.'

A short time later he was back on the Control Deck, wearing the heavy-duty equipment-slung survival suit used for planetary landings. Beside him stood Ponti, who was tall and dark, and the stocky fair-haired De Haan, both similarly equipped.

Salamar delivered a final briefing. 'The descent chamber's almost ready. The Probe will remain in orbit in case emergency escape procedures are needed. Keep in contact with me from the time you land.'

De Haan nodded alertly. 'Understood, Commander.'

'Your descent area is the one originally used by

Sorenson and his party. They won't have moved far, and you should have no difficulty in locating their base.'

'Unless something gets in our way,' Vishinsky spoke cynically. He couldn't help feeling irritated by Salamar's confident assumption that everything would go exactly according to plan. In Vishinsky's experience, things very seldom did.

Salamar's reaction was entirely predictable. 'You are both trained and equipped to deal with all contingencies. The purpose of this mission is to locate Professor Sorenson's survey team.' He paused, giving Vishinsky a challenging look. 'If there *are* hostile forces operating on Zeta Minor, we have the capacity to eliminate them!'

There came a bleeping signal from the console. 'Chamber's ready,' said Vishinsky. 'Let's get on with it.' He gave Salamar a sketchy salute and led his party out of the control room along the corridor, and into the dispatch chamber. A transparent door closed after them, the dispatch technician adjusted controls, and the three figures faded and vanished. Their molecules were dispersed, dispatched down a force-beam, re-assembled—and seconds later they were standing in the middle of the jungle.

Vishinsky looked round. 'Everyone O.K.? Right, check your blasters, and take off the safety.' He looked at the other two. Good men both of them, but young and inexperienced—like Salamar. Sternly Vishinsky said, 'I'd better warn you now, I don't share our Con-

troller's sunny optimism. On an alien planet you survive by treating everything as hostile until you know better. Understood? Now, let's take a look around.'
The three men moved off through the jungle.

The Doctor and Sarah reached the edge of the clearing. On the far side they could see the silent survival dome. Sarah looked questioningly at the Doctor. After a moment he nodded, and they started to move cautiously forward. Halfway across the clearing Sarah stumbled over something in the gloom. At first she took it for a log, then she looked more closely and jumped back horrified. At her feet lay the body of a man.

It was easy to see why she hadn't recognised what it was—the corpse was dry and twisted like an old tree branch. But it was a man right enough, a blaster-rifle clenched in one withered claw. They knelt down to examine it. The body was desiccated, almost mummified. Sarah shuddered and turned away. 'It looks like we're too late.'

'Several months too late, by the look of this poor chap,' said the Doctor thoughtfully.

Sarah pointed at the line of mounds before the dome. 'Doctor, those look like . . .'

'Graves? Yes, they do, don't they?'

The five mounds were an eerie sight in the half-light of the clearing. 'Five graves,' whispered Sarah. 'Five graves, and a dead body.' She wondered if the man they'd found had gone mad and killed his fellows, then starved to death himself. The Doctor was already on his way to the dome, and Sarah ran after him, following him inside.

Inside the dome it was even darker. Sarah could just about make out the shape of a control panel near the door. The Doctor shouted, 'Anybody about?' There was no reply.

'Can't we have some lights?' Sarah asked nervously.

The Doctor examined the control panel. 'The power seems to have run down.'

'Maybe that accounts for the weak signal.'

'Possibly, Sarah—ah!' The Doctor pointed to a red button. 'Here it is—an automatic distress button. High capacity power cells, dependent on sunlight for charging.' The Doctor was talking to himself. 'So why hasn't the sun kept them topped up?' He answered his own question. 'Obviously this planet's sun is too weak to do the job.'

Sarah tried to follow the Doctor's logic. 'So are we still in the solar system?'

'We're in *a* solar system, Sarah. But which particular sun provides the light and energy ...' The Doctor shrugged. 'Wherever we are, I think it's a very long way out.'

Sarah looked round the silent dome. 'What happened to everyone?'

'Well, what can we deduce from the facts at our disposal? This dome was clearly the base for some kind of scientific expedition. Possibly geological—remember that tool we found? Something went wrong, they sent out a distress signal ...'

'And died before help could arrive?'

The Doctor nodded. 'Something like that ... a lost expedition.'

'So what are we going to do now? Go back to the TARDIS and go home?' asked Sarah hopefully.

'We can't. Not until we know where we are. Besides, there may still be survivors—wandering around lost in that jungle.'

'We can't search a whole planet, Doctor.'

'No ... but if we go back to the TARDIS, and fetch my spectromixer, I can fix our position by the stars. And there are probably some spare power cells somewhere in this dome. I could get the communicator working and try to call up any survivors!'

Sarah sighed. She might have known they wouldn't just be going home. Things were never that simple— not with the Doctor. 'Wouldn't it save time if you got the communicator working and *I* went back to the TARDIS and got the spectromixer? I know where it is.'

The Doctor beamed. 'Would you do that, Sarah?' He took the TARDIS key from round his neck, and held it for a moment, making the telepathic adjustment that would allow Sarah to use it. He handed it to her. 'Sure you can find the way?'

'I think so. Across the clearing, then just follow the track.'

'Good thinking. Well, what are you waiting for?'

'The key.'

'Oh yes! Here you are.' The Doctor handed over the

key, and then took the tool they'd found from his pocket. 'You'd better take this too, just in case you run into anything hungry.'

'All right. See you!' Axe-hammer in one hand, key in the other, Sarah set off bravely into the night.

Left alone in the dome, the Doctor went on examining the control console. He pressed a button almost at random, and a section of wall slid slowly back. Behind it was what had obviously been the expedition's living and sleeping quarters. Tables, chairs, camp-beds, a litter of personal possessions ... It all looked reassuringly normal, as if the occupiers had just stepped out for a stroll. But as the sliding door drew fully back it revealed something else ... a huddled shape, at the edge of the door. Swiftly the Doctor crossed to examine it. Another body, wizened, twisted, almost mummified —just like the one outside in the clearing.

The Doctor became aware of a faint, incongruous sound. He froze, listening. He could hear *ticking*. He traced the sound to the big chronometer on the body's wrist. It was the old-fashioned sort, the kind that had to be wound up. The Doctor checked the winding stud. It would hardly turn. The dead man's watch was still going—and almost fully wound. Which meant that despite the appearance of the corpse, the man had died just a short time ago ...

The Doctor considered going after Sarah, but rejected the idea. What she didn't know wouldn't make her any more frightened. The Doctor decided he'd fix their position, get the communicator going and do his best to contact any survivors. Then he'd get them away from this mysterious and deadly planet just as fast as he could.

Sarah was already regretting her boldness as she stumbled through the darkness of the jungle. Several times she wandered off the track and had to cast about till she found it again. The jungle seemed to press in around her in a decidedly hostile fashion. Worse still, she couldn't shake off the feeling that she was being followed. Several times she heard faint sounds of movement behind her, though there was never anything to be seen by the time she swung round. Sarah decided she was suffering from nerves, told herself not to be silly and pressed grimly on. The square blue shape of the TARDIS appeared at last, and she broke into a run. She opened the door with the Doctor's key and disappeared thankfully inside.

As the door closed behind her, three shapes appeared out of the jungle. Vishinsky, Ponti and De Haan, all three with blasters levelled. They moved cautiously up to the TARDIS. They walked all round it, came to the front again and stood looking at each other in bafflement. Ponti stretched out a hand to the door. 'Don't touch it,' snapped Vishinsky. 'It may be booby-trapped.' He took out his communicator. 'Vishinsky to Controller.'

Salamar's voice crackled from the little speaker. 'Controller here. Report!'

Briefly Vishinsky told of the alien they'd tracked

through the jungle, and of the mysterious blue box into which it had disappeared.

On the Control Deck of the Probe, Salamar stood considering. He spoke into the microphone. 'Report understood. You have acted correctly, Vishinsky. Do not, repeat not, attempt to force entry.'

'Shall we disintegrate it?'

'Negative. It may yield essential information on hostile alien forces.'

He paused for a moment. 'Your orders are—seal off the object ready for transposition back to the Probe.' He spoke to the transposition technician on the intercom. 'Prepare to transport dangerous alien artefact from planet surface. You'd better prepare a quarantine berth to receive it. Vishinsky will give you the co-ordinates.'

Outside the TARDIS, Vishinsky and the others took small spray-guns from their belt kits and directed them at the TARDIS. In an incredibly short time it was sealed in a clear plastic coating.

Sarah found the spectromixer at last, after a long and frustrating search through the jumble of the Doctor's tool-locker. She closed the locker and operated the switch that opened the door. Nothing happened. She tried again. Still nothing. Sarah frowned. Either the TARDIS had gone wrong again—or something was keeping her inside ...

Vishinsky and the others stood well clear of the TARDIS. Vishinsky spoke into the communicator.

'Alien object prepared for transposition. Lock-on power beam and transmit.' Wrapped up in plastic like a supermarket chicken, the TARDIS silently disappeared.

In the silence that followed, Vishinsky heard a faint movement behind him. He spun round, blaster levelled. 'Something moved—just there!' Immediately two other blasters were trained on the same spot.

Vishinsky took a pace forward. 'Approach and identify yourself.' His voice hardened. 'This is your only warning. Whoever you are, come out now—or we fire!'

3

Meeting with a Monster

A strange dishevelled figure stumbled out of the jungle and stood blinking at them. It wore space coveralls so tattered and grimy as to be almost rags. Its eyes were red-rimmed with fatigue and a stubble of beard covered the grimy cheeks. Vishinsky had to look long and hard at this extraordinary figure before he realised it was the distinguished scientist he had come to find. 'Professor Sorenson!'

For all his outlandish appearance, Sorenson spoke in the formal precise tones of the academic. 'I have been observing you for some time. One has to be very careful on this planet. Appearances can be deceptive.'

Vishinsky looked hard at him. Despite the calm sensible tone of this remark, there was something very odd about Sorenson's manner. A suggestion of great pressures, of feverish excitement held under tight control. And surely Sorenson's speech had been *too* calm, *too* precise? Some show of human emotion would have been more natural—even from a leading scientist.

In the same dry, precise voice, Sorenson went on. 'It's the nights, you see. The days are quite safe ... but the nights ...' A shadow of fear passed across his face.

Vishinsky stared at him. 'Are you all right, Professor? Mission Control received no reports from your expedition. They sent us to investigate.'

'I am well, thank you,' said Sorenson politely. 'Indeed, I am more than well. My theories about Zeta Minor have been confirmed. Only last night I made the final discovery. My geological investigations in sector five, the area we called the Black Pool, have proved conclusively that . . .'

Vishinsky cut across the flow of words. This was no time for a lecture. 'Where are the others, Professor?'

'What? Oh, Baldwin returned to base. He was suffering from—from fatigue. Doubtless he has recovered by now. Come, I'll take you to the dome.'

As they set off through the jungle, Vishinsky said gently, 'There were *eight* in your party, Professor.'

Sorenson nodded vaguely. 'Indeed there were. We've had quite a few difficulties. This is a dangerous planet, you know. We've lost men, it's true. But the important thing is that my mission has been a success. I found what we came to find.'

Vishinsky could hardly believe his ears. Sorenson was dismissing the loss of his fellow scientists as if they'd been no more than mislaid pieces of equipment. 'How *many* men have you lost?'

Sorenson stopped and turned round. He stared desperately at Vishinsky and seemed to be struggling to speak. Then his face cleared, and he spoke in his usual calm manner, replying not to Vishinsky's question, but to a quite different one. 'No, it's all right, I'll be fine now. I just need a good rest. We haven't far to go.' He set off again through the jungle.

Ponti and De Haan stared at him in astonishment. Ponti seemed about to speak, but Vishinsky held a finger to his lips for silence. A theory was forming in Vishinsky's mind. Something had happened to the rest of Sorenson's expedition. Something so ghastly that the only way Sorenson could hang on to his sanity was by pretending that it hadn't happened at all ...

Vishinsky led the others after Sorenson. He wondered what they would find at the end of their journey.

The Doctor finished his examination of Baldwin's body, and stood contemplating it with growing concern. If the corpse had been laying here for months, even years, its condition would still have been puzzling enough. But if the man had died in the last few hours ... then whatever had killed him had instantly reduced his body to a mummified husk. The Doctor could think of only one possibility—a possibility so alarming he scarcely liked to contemplate it. And thinking of time ... surely Sarah should be back by now? The Doctor heard movements approaching the dome, and assumed she'd arrived at last. Then he realised that he was hearing the arrival of not one but a number of people. As he straightened up there was a sudden rush of footsteps. The Doctor found himself facing three grim-faced uniformed men.

A fourth figure, grimy and tattered, appeared from behind them and stared down at the body on the floor.

As he looked at Baldwin's body, Sorenson's unnatural self-control suddenly collapsed. His face crumpled, and his voice came out as a hysterical scream. 'It's Baldwin! He's dead ... murdered like all the others!'

The Doctor took a pace forward and three blasters came up to cover him. In a cold voice, Vishinsky snapped, 'You! Stay exactly where you are!'

The TARDIS stood in a bare metal-walled enclosure, with a viewing window set high on one wall. From behind the thick protective glass Salamar stood looking thoughtfully at the square blue box. Morelli, the Probe's Scientific Officer, was beside him. 'We've scanned it thoroughly, of course, Controller. The interior is shielded in some fashion. But photonic analysis of the exterior indicates elements similar to relics discovered on Terra in the second era.'

Salamar said incredulously, 'Earthlings? That's impossible. Terra has been uninhabited since the start of the third era.'

'Perhaps these aliens have been hiding out on a secret base there?'

Salamar became impatient with speculation. 'According to Vishinsky, there is an alien inside the thing. Remove the transportation seal.'

'You're going to let it out, Controller?'

'Yes. After all, if it's aggressive, we can always destroy it!'

Morelli touched a control, and a fine spray dissolved the plastic covering.

Sarah was fiddling desperately with the door controls. To her surprise, the door suddenly opened. She snatched up the axe-hammer and ran outside. She stopped in astonishment at the sight of her changed surroundings. Instead of dark alien jungle she was in a brightly-lit, high-walled metal room. She could dimly make out the forms of two men looking at her from a window high in the wall. Seconds later she realised something else. The room was airless. A metallic voice boomed, 'Do not move!'

Sarah said hoarsely. 'I can't *breathe* ...' She tried to go back to the TARDIS, but the door had closed, and she collapsed beside it, gasping for breath.

Salamar studied the writhing figure for a moment. 'A female. And clearly an oxygen-breather like ourselves.' He turned to Morelli. 'Transflow oxygen to quarantine area.'

There was a low hiss as air was pumped into the room below. They saw the alien female take deep gasping breaths and struggle to sit up. A light flashed and Morelli said, 'They're calling you on the Command Deck, Controller.'

Salamar turned to go. 'Very well. Complete quarantine procedures and bring the alien to me for interrogation.'

'That's right, a second alien. Calls himself the Doctor. Claims he landed here in response to a distress call.'

Salamar's voice came from the Probe. 'Have you checked the transmitters?'

'Yes. Power's almost gone. But if there was a signal

34

it would have been monitored by our receivers.'

'Perhaps my receivers are better than your receivers,' suggested the Doctor.

Ponti jabbed him with a blaster. 'Silence!'

'My manners certainly are,' concluded the Doctor reproachfully.

On the Command Deck, Salamar bit his lip in momentary indecision. For a moment he felt overwhelmed by the baffling turn of events, the constant demands for new and more difficult decisions. 'Can't Sorenson tell you what's been going on?' he snapped irritably.

'Negative,' crackled Vishinsky's voice. 'He's still in shock. His mental state seems to be strained.'

Salamar sighed. 'I suppose it's understandable. What about the alien prisoner?'

'Keeps on repeating the same story. He came to answer a distress signal and that's all he knows.'

A door slid open and Sarah was brought in under guard. Salamar looked thoughtfully at her. 'All right, Vishinsky, stand by for further orders. Maybe I'll have more success with *my* prisoner.'

Beside the Black Pool there was silence except for the sound of thick vegetation rustling in the night wind. Then something began to happen. There was a faint crackling sound on the night air. Dust swirled and vegetation waved wildly as something vast, invisible and alien, emerged from the Black Pool and began moving through the jungle.

Salamar's interrogation wasn't having the success for which he'd hoped. The alien, although young and female, seemed tougher than she looked. She spoke up for herself spiritedly, and seemed unimpressed by threats and attempts to frighten her. Angrily he returned to the attack. 'You were found in possession of a geological hammer of Morestran design—the type that was issued to the missing expedition.'

'We picked it up in the jungle.'

'Just as you "picked up" this mysterious distress signal?'

'That's right. How many times do I have to tell you?'

Salamar's voice was scornful. 'Do you have any idea where Zeta Minor is situated?'

'No,' said Sarah wearily.

Salamar paused impressively. 'It is beyond Cygnus A. It is as distant again from the centre of the Artoro Galaxy as that Galaxy is from the Anterides. It is on the *very edge* of the known universe—and you just happened to be passing!'

'We were on our way back to Earth,' said Sarah desperately.

Salarmar pounced. 'But you said you *came* from Earth.'

Sarah sighed. This young Controller cut a handsome figure in his fancy uniform, but he had a nasty suspicious mind for all that. It was so unfair, thought Sarah bitterly. Why should she have to struggle with all the impossible explanations, just because the Doctor had decided to play good Samaritan?

Wearily she launched on yet another explanation,

conscious before she began that no one was going to believe her. 'We were on our way back to Earth, when something went wrong. The Doctor picked up this signal and ...'

She was interrupted by a beep from the Control Console. Salamar turned away from her and snapped, 'Yes?'

'Morelli, Captain. Decision to land on planet or remain in orbit will soon be imperative.'

Impulsively Salamar said, 'We'll go in now. Prepare for landing.' He'd just have to go down and sort things out himself. He turned back to Sarah. 'I think you and your companion know far more about Zeta Minor than you want us to think. I shall confront you with your fellow-conspirator and get the truth from you both. Take her away.'

Sarah was hustled out, and Salamar swung round to the duty flight-officer. 'Commence landing procedure.'

The landing procedure operated smoothly, and the Morestran Probe settled down to a soft landing on the edge of the jungle, in the clearing next to the expedition's survival dome. Very soon Controller Salamar was leading a small party consisting of himself, Sarah and a couple of guards into the dome, where Vishinsky was waiting with his prisoner.

The Doctor and Sarah were given no time for a reunion. Sarah was thrust into the sealed-off living quarters, now converted to a temporary prison, while Salamar started his investigation by interrogating Sorenson.

After his sudden breakdown, Sorenson had returned to a more normal state of mind. The arrival of the relief expedition had restored his grip on reality. At last he was able to admit the terrible sequence of events on Zeta Minor—rather than, as before, taking refuge in a pretence that they had never happened. Now he was giving Salamar a fairly rational account of what had happened to his expedition. 'We'd only been working a few weeks. Just after we'd started the preliminary surveys, Lorenzo went. The next was Gurn, and then Summers . . .'

Salamar nodded towards a corner where Baldwin's body, now shrouded in plastic, lay waiting for return to the ship.

'They all died in the same way?'

Sorenson nodded. 'For a while it stopped. We thought we were safe, that . . . whatever it was . . . had decided to leave us in peace. But it wasn't to be. Ericson was next . . . then Lumb . . . There was another lull. Braun, Baldwin and myself were the only ones left. We went on with the work—it seemed the only thing to do . . .' He looked wonderingly at them, seeming to realise the truth at last. 'They're all dead—and I'm the only survivor . . .' His voice broke, and he buried his face in his hands.

Gently Vishinsky asked, 'Why didn't you send a call for help?'

'We did. But the power cells were low. And something about this planet seems to muffle communications except for very short distances.'

'And these attacks—they all happened at night?'

Sorenson nodded. 'Yes ... the nights are the worst time ...' He gazed fearfully at the door of the dome, as if expecting some terrifying monster to appear out of the darkness.

Salamar said impatiently, 'Surely that's obvious, Vishinsky? Any force of alien infiltrators is naturally going to operate under cover of dark.' He glared threateningly at the Doctor. 'I advise you to make an immediate and full confession. It will save you a great deal of discomfort.'

Bluntly the Doctor said, 'Discomfort? You mean you're going to torture me?'

Salamar winced at the Doctor's directness. 'We are going to interrogate you, Doctor. But I warn you, nobody resists Morestran interrogation for very long.' He turned to a guard. 'Put him with the girl. Maybe she can convince him to be sensible.'

Vishinsky touched a control and the door to the living quarters slid back, revealing an anxiously waiting Sarah. The Doctor was thrust in with her, and the door closed behind them.

With the Doctor out of the way, some of Salamar's brash self-assurance seemed to diminish. He looked worriedly at Vishinsky. 'We must try to contact the home planet again, ask for instructions.'

'You heard what the Professor said, Controller—this far out, we're on our own.'

Salamar stood undecided for a moment, then looked up sharply as Ponti and De Haan came back into the dome. 'Well?'

Ponti shrugged and spread his hands. 'We've

searched a wide belt of jungle in all directions. No sign of hostile life.'

All three of his subordinates looked inquiringly at Salamar, and he felt a sudden surge of panic. Fighting it down, he took refuge, as usual, in arbitrary decision. 'So that narrows the killer down to our two alien prisoners. Execute them immediately.'

Vishinsky was about to protest, but before he could speak Salamar ended all discussion. 'I shall return to the Probe. Professor Sorenson, you'd better come with me—I want medicare to take a look at you.'

An ear pressed to the thin metal partition, the Doctor reacted with indignation. 'We've just been condemned to death, Sarah. We'd better do something quickly!'

Sarah tried the metal-framed window, and to her astonishment it moved under her touch. 'Let's just clear off then, shall we?'

'How?'

'Through here!' Sarah indicated the window.

The Doctor looked incredulously at her. It seemed astonishing that their captors could have been so careless. Then he grinned. 'Of course, magnetic locks. And the power's so low they're not operating!' He pushed the window fully open. 'Come on, Sarah, what are we waiting for?' They climbed out into the darkness.

The massive shape of the Morestran spaceship towered high above the dome, guards patrolling around it.

The Doctor set off through the jungle, but Sarah

40

tugged at his sleeve. 'Where do you think you're off to, Doctor?'

'Back to the TARDIS, of course. We won't help anyone by getting ourselves executed.'

'Well, you're heading the wrong way. The TARDIS is on board that spaceship.'

'Ah!' The Doctor paused, rubbing his chin. 'Then we'd better get on board ourselves. Once we're inside the TARDIS we can be away in no time. Now then, Sarah, if you distract that guard by the ramp, I can slip up behind him and put him gently to sleep . . .'

The Doctor's plans were interrupted by a strange crackling sound. It was coming out of the darkness of the jungle and moving rapidly closer. It seemed to be rushing towards them at amazing speed. Sarah's eyes widened and she started stumbling dazedly towards the source of the sound. The Doctor grabbed her and pulled her down.

'Back, Sarah. Keep back!'

They ducked into the shadows at the side of the dome. The sound became louder, and louder still, until it seemed to fill the air. Sarah screamed and pointed. *Something* huge, shapeless and entirely horrible was rolling out of the jungle towards them.

4

Tracked by the Oculoid

The Doctor looked up at the monstrous apparition. He found it curiously hard to decide exactly *what* he was seeing. It was huge and menacing—its cloudy form outlined in shimmering red. The shape was constantly changing, like that of a storm-cloud in the sky. Sometimes it seemed like a dragon with fangs and claws, sometimes it was just a formless mass. There was a terrifying quality of *otherness* about it, as if it didn't belong on this world, or on any world in the universe. The Doctor felt he was looking at a creature from some other dimension. The sound that accompanied it was alien too, a high-pitched crackle that seemed to vibrate across every nerve in his body.

The guard in front of the spaceship stared up at the apparition in horrified fascination. He raised his blaster-rifle and fired bolt after bolt into the threatening mass. The results were immediate and terrifying. The crackling noise rose to an angry shriek and the red-outlined mass seemed to swoop down on the guard, sucking his writhing figure into its own invisible nothingness. Struggling and screaming, the guard disappeared.

The sound faded, and the shimmering outline

moved away into the jungle. Ponti and De Haan ran from the dome and stood staring wildly around them.

'There's nothing here,' said Ponti incredulously. He looked across at the spaceship. 'Who's the guard on this sector?'

'O'Hara. But there's no sign of him.'

Ponti stared round the clearing, failing to see the Doctor and Sarah crouched in the darkness beneath the window. 'We need some lights around here. You look for O'Hara, I'll get the power-packs.'

As the two men disappeared round the side of the dome, the Doctor pulled Sarah to her feet. 'Come on, we'd better get moving.'

They heard the crackling again, and Sarah froze in terror. 'Doctor, it's coming back ...'

The crackling grew louder, there was a strangely horrible 'plop', and the withered body of the guard dropped out of nothingness on to the ground. The sound moved away, and the Doctor saw a faint shimmer of red through the jungle as it disappeared. The Doctor whispered, 'I think it's really gone this time.' Sarah was crouching with her hands over her face. Gently he lifted her to her feet. 'Sarah ... what's the matter?'

She stared wildly at him. 'I don't know. I felt as if I was being drawn out of my body.' She shuddered. 'It's the same feeling I had before, that time in the jungle.'

'I think you've had a very narrow escape.' The Doctor went to the body of the guard and knelt to examine it.

Sarah tried not to look. 'Doctor ... what do you think that thing was?'

'I don't know. But I've got a *very* unpleasant theory.' Totally absorbed, the Doctor went on with his examination.

Inside the dome, everything was panic and confusion. They had all heard the crackling sound, the noise of blaster fire, the screams of the guard, and Ponti and De Haan had run out to investigate. At the same time the lights in the dome had dimmed almost to nothingness. Now, just as mysteriously, they had come on again. Vishinsky checked the controls. 'Everything's normal now. But *something* caused a sudden massive power-drain. There was a temperature drop of several degrees.'

Ponti ran back into the dome. 'I think we're under attack, Controller. There was this weird sound out there—and O'Hara's disappeared.'

Suddenly Salamar shouted, 'Vishinsky! Check the prisoners!'

Vishinsky operated the control, and the door slid back to reveal empty living quarters and the open window.

'As I thought,' said Salamar bitterly. 'They've escaped—or been rescued by their friends.'

Vishinsky grabbed his communicator. 'I'll put the crew on full alert. Ponti, get out there and organise a search. I'll send help from the ship.'

Ponti grabbed a portable searchlight and called to

the guards. 'You two—come with me.' They ran out into the night.

The Doctor was still examining the body. Nervously Sarah said, 'Come on, Doctor, they're sure to miss us soon.'

'This is quite fascinating, Sarah. It's like those other poor fellows. It's as though the very life-force has been sucked out of the body.'

A sudden blinding light appeared, moving towards them. They heard shouts and the footsteps of running men. 'I think they *have* missed us,' said the Doctor solemnly. 'Come on, Sarah, run for it!' They sprinted across the clearing and into the jungle. Blaster-bolts sizzled over their heads as the guards opened fire.

As soon as they were under cover, the Doctor tripped Sarah and flung himself flat beside her. The beam of the searchlight swept over their heads, and they heard the sound of pursuit moving off in a different direction. The Doctor tapped Sarah's shoulder, and they began wriggling cautiously away from the dome.

Inside the dome Salamar paced angrily up and down. Vishinsky, who had been examining the open window, came back towards him. 'Pretty obvious what happened, Controller. The power-drain weakened the magnetic locks and they cleared off through the window.'

'Well, of course it's obvious,' snarled Salamar. 'But

how did they cause the power-drain? Did they manage some kind of sabotage, or have they got friends lurking out there?'

Ponti hurried in. 'We spotted them, Controller, but they got away into the jungle. And—there's something you ought to see for yourself, sir. They've killed O'Hara.'

He led them out of the dome and across the clearing, to the mummified body of O'Hara. Salamar looked at it in horrified anger. 'They must be recaptured. They must be made to pay!'

Ponti looked dubious. 'We'll never find them in the jungle at night.'

'Then we'll launch the Oculoid at dawn. They won't escape *that*!'

'Very good, Controller.'

Salamar looked down at the body. 'Vishinsky, I want Professor Sorenson to see this.'

'Is that wise, Controller? He's still under medicare in the Probe.'

'Get him! And tell the medics I want a full bio-analysis on the body.' Salamar stalked away.

Vishinsky looked after him, a cynical smile on his lips. His brilliant young Controller was learning that there was more to commanding than wearing a fancy uniform. He wondered how long Salamar would hold up under the strain.

The Doctor and Sarah were forcing their way through a particularly tangled stretch of jungle. The Doctor had made for the thickest cover, which inevitably meant the area where the going was hardest. Thorns snatched at their clothing, vines and creepers tangled their feet. Sarah stumbled blindly forward, holding on to the end of the Doctor's scarf as a kind of safety line. She got caught in a clump of thorns, the Doctor went on moving forward, and the scarf tightened until it nearly throttled him. He let out an indignant squawk, and loosened the scarf round his throat. 'What are you doing back there, Sarah?'

'I'm doing my best,' said Sarah indignantly. 'It's all so dark and tangled, Doctor. Where are we going?'

The Doctor made his way back, and disentangled her. 'My dear Sarah,' he began—then suddenly swept her to the ground and into the shelter of some dense bushes. Sarah started to protest but the Doctor put his hand over her mouth. 'Ssh! Listen!'

A sound was coming towards them. A strange alien crackling sound, which seemed to set their nerves quivering. Sarah thought of the withered body of the guard, and lay very quiet and very still.

The sound came nearer . . . nearer . . . then seemed to pass by. They got slowly to their feet, and Sarah gave a sigh of relief. 'That was pretty lucky.'

The Doctor glanced up at the sky, which was showing the faintest hint of pale blue light. 'Night's candles are burnt out,' he said poetically. 'And jocund day stands tiptoe on the misty mountain top. Or something like that!'

'What? Oh I get it, Shakespeare! You mean it's getting light?'

'That's what Shakespeare meant.'

'And that ... thing ... doesn't like daylight?'

The Doctor replied with another quotation. '*That* is the question!' He set off in the direction of the sound.

'Doctor, where are you going?' called Sarah in alarm.

The Doctor didn't reply, but kept striding on.

Sarah looked up at the sky. It was certainly getting lighter. Hoping the Doctor was right about the monster's nocturnal habits, she hurried after him.

The coming of dawn was also registered in the Command Area of the Morestran Probe. Vishinsky looked across at Morelli, who was busy at the console. 'Trajectile chamber three ... ignition procedures ... activate!'

Morelli acknowledged the command. 'Trajectile chamber three ... activated. Oculoid function normal.'

A hatch opened in the exterior hull of the probe, and a strange-looking object emerged. It was wedge-shaped and its dominant feature was a very large forward-mounted lens, which made the thing look like a giant metal insect, with one huge eye. The resemblance was further increased by the angry buzzing sound of its anti-gravitational drive system. This was the Oculoid Tracker, one of the triumphs of Morestran technology. It hovered for a moment then, buzzing angrily, it rose in the air and set off over the jungle.

Its progress was controlled from inside the Command Area, where a small monitor screen showed whatever the Oculoid's vision-lens 'saw'. At the moment the screen showed a dense canopy of tree-tops with occasional gaps—the jungle seen from above.

'Launch attitude seven,' snapped Vishinsky. 'Telesystems on transverse sweep mode.'

'Transverse sweep established.'

'Maintain ocular frequencies.' Vishinsky turned as Salamar came into the control area. 'Oculoid Tracker launched, Controller.'

Salamar nodded but didn't speak. His eyes were fixed on the monitor screen.

The Doctor and Sarah were crossing one of the many small clearings that dotted the jungle, when Sarah heard the droning sound high overhead. She grabbed the Doctor's arm and pointed, and they both sprinted for the far side of the clearing. From the shelter of the trees they watched the strange-looking object hover overhead for a moment and then whirr away. 'What was that?' asked Sarah. 'An elfin spirit of the forest?'

She was rather pleased with this apt Shakespearean quotation, but the Doctor seemed to take it literally. 'No, no, Sarah, it's some kind of surveillance device.'

Sarah gave a rueful smile. 'Well, as long as someone knows where we are, I suppose we're not really lost.'

They moved on through the jungle. It seemed to be thinning out now, and the going was easier. The Doctor suddenly emerged from his reverie. 'I met him once, you know.'

'Who?'

'Shakespeare. Charming fellow, but a perfectly dreadful actor.'

By now Sarah was used to the casual familiarity with which the Doctor spoke of the most eminent historical figures. So she just nodded and said, 'Perhaps that's why he took up writing?'

'Yes,' said the Doctor thoughtfully. 'Yes, perhaps it was.' They trudged on through the jungle.

The monitor screen linked to the Oculoid Tracker continued to show an aerial view of the jungle, and since one patch of vegetation looked very like another, the Morestran crew soon stopped watching it. Morelli glanced casually at it from time to time to see if any thing new had shown up. Only Salamar still stood motionless, gazing unblinkingly at the little screen.

Ponti brought Professor Sorenson into the Command Area. The geologist looked pale and shaken. Salamar swung round. 'You've seen the body?'

Sorsenson nodded. 'Yes, I've seen it.'

'Well?'

'What can I tell you? All my party died the same way. But as to what killed them ...' Sorenson gave a helpless shrug.

Salamar tapped a plastic file. 'I have the bioanalysis here. All the organs are undamaged, no contusions or evidence of pressure. Complete extraction of bodily fluids from all tissues.'

Sorenson shrugged helplessly. 'Some kind of weapon, perhaps?'

'Then it's an alien one,' said Vishinsky grimly. 'There's nothing in our technology that could produce such an effect.'

Salamar nodded his agreement. 'A heat weapon would have produced external injuries. All the indications are that something like an incredibly rapid form of freeze-drying occurred.'

Sorenson waved the report away. 'Isn't all this largely irrelevant?'

Salamar glared at him in outrage, 'Irrelevant? What exactly do you mean, Professor?'

'I came to Zeta Minor to prove a theory that could save our entire civilisation. *And I have been successful!* That is all that matters.'

'Seven men—seven of your colleagues, Professor— have died on this planet, not to mention one of my crew ...'

Sorenson waved aside the deaths of his colleagues. 'There is more at stake here than a few lives. You know as well as I that our entire solar system is dependent on a dying sun. I have discovered a new and virtually inexhaustible energy-source ...'

Morelli's voice broke into the lecture. 'Commander, the Oculoid Tracker has located the prisoners.'

Salamar gave a grin of savage satisfaction. 'Send out a pursuit party immediately.'

As Vishinsky began snapping orders into the microphone, Sorenson drew Salamar aside. 'You're wasting time, Controller. All that concerns you now is to get my samples aboard and prepare for immediate take-off.'

Salamar said coldly. 'I am well aware of your high position on the Science Council, Professor. But this happens to be a military expedition with military objectives. Hostile alien forces must be searched out and destroyed whenever encountered. That operation is now in hand. We'll blast off when we've captured these alien murderers and executed them—and not before!'

5

The Lair of the Monster

The Doctor and Sarah stood at the brink of the Black Pool, staring down into its depths. 'Yes, this is it,' muttered the Doctor. 'It must be.' He began working his way around the rocky edge of the pool.

Sarah followed him. 'You mean this is where the thing lives?'

'It doesn't live anywhere—not in the sense you mean,' said the Doctor severely. 'It just *is*!'

Sarah heard a faint droning sound high overhead. She looked up and saw a metal shape above them. 'Doctor, look!'

The Doctor glanced up. 'Oh, never mind that wretched thing.' He returned his attention to the pool. 'Now then, Sarah, look down there. What do you see?'

'A pool.'

The Doctor sighed. 'All right then, what *don't* you see? Lean right over and look down.'

Nervously Sarah obeyed. The jet blackness seemed to absorb her gaze, drawing her forward. She heard the Doctor's voice. 'Wouldn't you expect to see some kind of reflection?'

Sarah gazed into the pool, realising the Doctor was right. The jet black surface ought to have acted as a perfect mirror. She should have seen her own face looking back at her. But instead she saw no glimmer of a reflection, no gleam of light. 'There's nothing,' she whispered. 'Nothing at all.' With an effort she drew back from the pool and stared up at the Doctor. She remembered his mysterious remark about the monster. 'What do you mean—it just *is*?'

Still gazing into the pool, the Doctor didn't reply. Sarah heard a rustle of movement behind her. She turned to see a group of Morestran guards emerging from the jungle. They grouped themselves in a semi-circle, blaster-rifles covering the Doctor and Sarah.

Ponti, who was in charge of the group, snapped, 'Raise your hands above your heads, both of you!' He had seen the murdered body of his friend O'Hara, and he was taking no chances.

The Doctor looked at the tense faces of the guards. These men were frightened, and therefore dangerous. Slowly he raised his hands, and Sarah did the same.

'Search them,' ordered Ponti.

The Doctor felt hands gripping his arms, and shook them off in a spurt of irritation. 'I'm quite prepared to empty my own pockets!'

Ponti immediately suspected some alien trick. 'We'll do the searching. Put your hands back above your head.'

'I assure you I've nothing up my sleeve, if that's what you're worried about. Now if you'll kindly treat us in a more civilised manner . . .'

Ponti lost patience. 'I said search them! And you needn't be too gentle.'

The guards closed in on the Doctor, he threw them off with surprising ease, and Ponti went to help subdue him. All this was happening on the very brink of the Black Pool. One of the guards tripped and stumbled backwards into Ponti, sending him reeling over the edge. Ponti's sudden scream was as suddenly cut off, as the pool's uncanny blackness absorbed him.

There was a shocked silence, and the struggling group of figures froze like statues. One of the guards made an involuntary movement to dive in and rescue Ponti, but the Doctor pulled him away. 'Get back! Get back, all of you!' The astonished guards obeyed.

The Doctor looked angrily at them. 'You people have interfered with the balance of nature on this planet in ways you don't understand. It may already be too late to undo the harm that's been done. Now take us to your ship. I must warn your Commander.'

The Doctor and Sarah set off, and the guards, thoroughly cowed, followed them meekly through the jungle.

In the deserted survival dome Sorenson was carefully taking a number of stubby metal canisters from his locker. Although Salamar had refused his demands for an immediate take-off, Sorenson was determined to collect his mineral samples from the dome and get them on board the ship. De Haan, who had been dragooned into helping him, looked on uninterestedly as Sorenson indicated the selected canisters. 'These are the most vital specimens. I want them loaded with the utmost care.'

De Haan spoke reassuringly. 'Don't worry, Professor, we'll look after them. What's inside?'

'Refined ore containing incredible amounts of potential energy.' Sorenson paused impressively. 'I calculate that six pounds of this material, taken back to our solar system, would produce energy equivalent to the output of our own sun over a period of three centuries.'

De Haan looked blankly at him, clearly unable to grasp the magnitude of Sorenson's claim. Sorenson felt a sudden spurt of irritation. This oaf was typical of the fools who surrounded him, all too wrapped up in their own petty concerns to appreciate true greatness.

'Don't you understand?' he shouted. 'Full-scale exploitation of this planet will provide us with a perpetual supply of energy in any quantity we need. I've made the greatest discovery in scientific history.'

De Haan wondered if the Professor was cracking up again. 'What about the rest of this stuff?'

Sorenson glanced round the dome where he and his colleagues had worked together, and endured so much. Now they were all dead. He turned away. 'You still don't understand the implications, do you?' he said wearily. 'No, there's nothing here. The base can be abandoned.'

Salamar sat brooding in his command chair, and looked up as Vishinsky entered. 'Well, are they here?'

'They've just cleared quarantine.'

'Weapons?'

'Our detectors reveal nothing. If they did cause all these deaths they must have used some extra-sensory process beyond our understanding.' Vishinsky paused. 'Ponti didn't make it back, Controller. I gather there was an accident ...' He told Salamar what had happened.

'Accident? You mean these aliens killed him. Where's Sorenson?'

'Getting his samples aboard ready for the launch.'

Salamar's fist hammered the arm of his chair. 'I have given no order for a launch. Nor shall I until I've accounted for these deaths.'

'Sorenson has a lot of influence in high circles,' warned Vishinsky. 'It may be unwise to antagonise him.'

'I am not entirely without influence myself. Sorenson is a civilian. Military affairs must always have precedence.'

A door slid back and the Doctor and Sarah appeared. Salamar sat straighter in his chair. 'Bring the prisoners forward!'

One of the prisoners was already forward. The Doctor's long legs carried him ahead so rapidly that his guards were left trailing behind, transformed into a sort of escort. He marched straight up to Salamar. 'What do you mean, prisoners? We're not prisoners, we came here to help!'

'You are prisoners of the Morestran Empire, and you are charged with acts of war including the murder of several Morestran subjects. How do you plead?'

'Not guilty,' said Sarah automatically. She suddenly realised this was not an English courtroom but an alien spaceship. 'Oh, this is ridiculous!'

'Silence,' ordered Vishinsky.

The Doctor ignored him. 'Have you people any idea just what you've come up against on this planet?'

Salamar jumped to his feet in rage. 'You will not evade my questions with counter-questions!'

The Doctor looked coolly at the angry young man before him. Clearly the poor fellow was on the verge of hysteria. 'Now look here, old chap ...' he began in a soothing voice.

Vishinsky felt obliged to come to the support of his Controller. 'Silence!' he ordered again. 'You will be given a chance to speak in due course.'

Trembling with rage Salamar sank back into his chair. 'This is an official interrogation, and it will be conducted in an orderly manner,' he shouted. He gestured to the guards who raised their blaster-rifles. 'Failure to co-operate will result in your *immediate* execution.'

The Doctor sighed. 'So, if I tell you the truth, you won't believe me—and if I don't you'll kill me ...'

Sorenson hovered anxiously as his precious canisters were stacked in the quarantine chamber beside the TARDIS. Morelli checked a radiation-detector. 'They're radioactive all right, but well within our tolerance-level. What's inside them, Professor?'

'Mineral elements,' said Sorenson. 'Mineral elements from the planet. They're of the greatest scientific importance.'

The interrogation was now proceeding on more orderly lines, with Salamar well-launched on a long speech of accusation. 'You were first discovered beside the body of one of our scientists. Last night one of our guards died—and again you were seen kneeling over him. Can you or can you not explain this?'

'Yes, of course I can! These deaths, and the others which preceded them, all came about because of your people's interference on this planet.' The Doctor looked round at the circle of suspicious faces. 'Don't you realise? Here on Zeta Minor is the boundary between existence as you know it and ...' The Doctor paused, wondering how to put it in a way they could understand. '... And that *other* universe which your minds cannot comprehend.'

Most of the Morestrans reacted with baffled suspicion—all except Vishinsky. His practical mind had long ago realised that there was something very strange about this planet. Something which couldn't be explained away by Salamar's convenient theories of mysteriously hostile aliens with super-weapons. 'Another universe, Doctor?'

The Doctor was using all his powers of persuasion. 'Yes,' he said urgently. 'Another universe. It has existed from the beginning, side by side with the known universe ... each the total antithesis of the other. You call it nothingness—a meaningless word to cover ignorance. Thousands of years ago, Earth scientists had another word for it. They called it anti-matter.'

There was a stunned silence in the Command Area. Salamar said uncertainly, 'It's all nonsense. Mumbojumbo and deception, to cover their real motives.'

Vishinsky looked thoughtful. 'Maybe so. But let him finish.'

Impressively the Doctor continued. 'By coming here, you have crossed the boundary into that other universe and plundered it. An incredibly dangerous and foolish thing to do . . .'

Sorenson blundered into the Command Area, too obsessed with his own concerns to notice what was going on. 'Controller Salamar! My mineral samples are now on board, and we must take off immediately!' He blinked and stared round, suddenly realising the Command Area seemed unusually crowded.

The Doctor said sternly, 'Professor Sorenson, you cannot take any part of this planet away with you.'

Sorenson spluttered, 'Well, of course I can. That was the whole purpose of my expedition.'

The Doctor was almost tearing his hair in sheer exasperation. 'You still don't understand, do you? It's not just that you *shouldn't* do it. You *can't* do it.'

Salamar, meanwhile, was furious—no one seemed to be taking any notice of him. As usual he took refuge in one of his arbitrary decisions. 'Take the prisoners away,' he ordered. 'I'll deal with them later. The inquiry is suspended.'

As they were hustled out, the Doctor called back, 'If

you don't listen to me, Salamar, you'll never be allowed to leave this planet!' The door closed behind him, muffling his still-protesting voice.

As soon as he was gone, Salamar rounded on Sorenson. 'Now see here, Professor Sorenson, I am well aware of your scientific importance. But *I* am in command of this Probe and *I* decide when the ship takes off. Do you understand?'

To Salamar's fury, Sorenson scarcely seemed to be listening. 'Yes, yes, of course,' he said absently, still gazing at the door through which the struggling Doctor had departed. 'I wonder what he meant—saying we'll never be *allowed* to leave ...'

The Doctor and Sarah were marched along corridors and finally thrust into the quarantine area where Sarah had first been held prisoner. The door closed behind them.

Sarah looked at the Doctor, who was gazing abstractedly around him, hands thrust deep into his pockets. 'Don't you ever get tired of being pushed around?'

'Frequently!'

Sarah patted the side of the TARDIS. 'So why don't we just go inside and disappear?'

'I'm afraid we can't do that, Sarah. Mind you, they're so stubborn it's tempting to let them go ahead and destroy themselves. The trouble is, they wouldn't be the only ones. They could set off a chain reaction that might lead to cataclysm.'

'The big bang?'

'The biggest, Sarah. The end of the universe.'

Sarah nodded resignedly. Somehow she'd known all along that they weren't simply going to clear off. Things were never that simple.

The Doctor had wandered across to the pile of metal canisters, and was examining them curiously. He picked one up and started unscrewing the lid. 'Now what have we here, I wonder?' He took off the lid and peered inside.

The walls of the canister were very thick, so that the actual storage area was small. The canister was filled with a fine reddish dust. The Doctor tipped a little out on to the upturned lid. 'You remember the look of the rocks around the pool, Sarah?'

'Sort of reddish-brown?'

'This is a concentrated form of the same mineral substance. You can see it's the same colour.'

Sarah looked closely at the powder. 'Not any more it isn't,' she said suddenly. 'It's changing . . .'

They watched as the colour changed from red to green, then back again to red. The Doctor nodded thoughtfully and tipped the powder in the lid back into the canister. He fished in his pockets until he discovered a brightly-coloured little tin, containing one solitary piece of toffee, which he promptly ate. He tipped some of the red powder from the canister into the tin and stowed the tin back in his pocket. Then he screwed the lid back on the canister and replaced it with the others.

Sarah watched this strange performance with growing puzzlement. 'What on earth are you up to?'

'Just an idea, Sarah. After all, you never know what will come in useful, do you?'

There was a sudden low humming noise and the chamber began to vibrate. Sarah looked round in alarm. 'What's going on?'

'It's the compression units. They must be preparing to blast off.'

The Doctor slammed a fist into his palm. 'The idiots. They don't really think they'll be allowed to leave, do they? '

'What's going to stop them?'

'This is!' The Doctor pointed dramatically to the pile of canisters.

With an ordered bustle of activity, the take-off routines got under way. Salamar sat in his command chair, Vishinsky beside him. Despite his angry protests to Sorenson, Salamar really had no good reason *not* to take off. The fate of the expedition had been discovered, and the sole survivor was safely aboard, together with his precious samples. The prisoners could just as well be interrogated and executed on the home planet as on board the Probe Ship. Indeed there was something to be said for bringing them home in triumph.

Vishinsky began running through the final checks. 'Pressurisation complete. Activate cyclo-stimulators. Power jets to lock-in positions. Gyro-stabilisers activate. Prepare for final ignition. Ten, nine, eight ...'

Suddenly there was a terrible grinding noise and

the whole ship vibrated. 'Pressurisation falling,' shouted Morelli. 'Cyclo-stimulators no longer responding.'

Salamar leaned forward, studying the wildly flickering range of warning lights on the control console. 'Emergency procedure. Activate secondary launch units.'

Vishinsky's hands flickered over the controls. 'Secondary launch units activated.'

The groaning of the drive units continued, and Salamar stared unbelievingly at the instrument readings. 'I don't understand . . .' he muttered.

Neither did Vishinsky, but the Doctor's words kept coming back to his mind, *'You won't be allowed to leave.'*

Hovering nervously in the background Sorenson stammered, 'What's happening? What's gone wrong?'

His only answer was the panic-stricken voice of Morelli. 'Emergency power-units inoperative. Main and secondary units failing . . .'

Instinctively Vishinsky snapped, 'Cancel ignition.'

Morelli stabbed frantically at the controls and the groaning noise died away. Vishinsky gave a sigh of relief. He sensed that any further efforts at take-off would have blown the drive-units, and like every old space hand, his first concern was for the safety of the ship.

Salamar glanced angrily at his subordinate, but the order was so logical that he didn't dare to countermand it.

Vishinsky was studying the instrument readings in

total bafflement. 'It doesn't make sense . . .'

Suddenly the whole Probe shuddered, and a strange roaring sound came from outside the ship. Sorenson ran to a viewing port and shouted, 'Look!'

They all crowded round him. Outside the ship, a vast monstrous shape outlined in flickering blue light was lurching towards them. 'It's come back,' screamed Sorenson. 'It's going to attack the ship!'

6

The Battle for the Spaceship

Sorenson stared wonderingly out of the viewing port, his eyes alight with scientific interest. 'Incredible,' he breathed. 'Pure energy, yet with a kind of physical form!'

Vishinsky looked over his shoulder, studying the Monster. The flickering outline held suggestions of a dragon-like creature with powerful head and great clawed hands. Its outline glowed a fierce blue that reminded him of lightning, and its savage roaring filled the air.

Salamar turned away from the viewing port. 'Morelli, set up the force-field barrier. Someone bring the alien prisoners up here. They may know something about this.'

A guard ran to get the prisoners, while Morelli tried the force-field controls. 'The barrier won't work, Controller. There's some kind of a power-drain ...'

Salamar ran to the viewing port. The Monster was almost upon them now, its flickering talons reaching out for the ship. He turned to the nearest guard. 'Take an armed party out there and see if you can stop it.'

There was a hooting of alarm sirens and the pounding of booted feet on metal floors. Soon armed men were running down the ramp, blazing away with their rifles at the approaching menace.

Salamar and the others watched the battle from the viewing ports.

Blaster-fire had no effect on the shimmering monster, seeming merely to irritate it. It flowed forward and sucked in the men in the front rank, absorbing them into nothingness. The others fell back, still firing, and retreated to the safety of the ship.

The Doctor and Sarah were thrust back into the control room. The Doctor ran to the viewing port and took in the situation outside.

'You've sent those men to their deaths,' he said angrily. He turned from the window and leaned over the control console. 'Use the force-field barrier.'

Morelli shrugged helplessly. 'We've tried—there isn't enough power.'

'Then link it through to your atomic accelerator. That'll give you the extra power you need.'

'We can't do that—it's too dangerous.'

There came another shattering roar from outside, and a scream as yet another guard was engulfed. 'Things will get a lot more dangerous if you don't do it,' warned the Doctor. 'Now, link the force-field to the atomic accelerator. It's your only chance!'

Morelli instinctively looked at Salamar, who was biting his lip indecisively.

Vishinsky shouted, 'You've got to do it, Salamar. It's our only chance.'

Panic in his voice, Salamar screamed, 'All right, then. Do it!'

Morelli worked frantically at the console for a few moments and then glanced up. 'Link to accelerator complete.'

'Operate force-field,' ordered Vishinsky. They all ran to the viewing ports.

The Monster had almost reached the ship by now and the few surviving guards were retreating up the ramp. The Monster surged forward—and suddenly hit the invisible barrier of the force-field. There was a fierce crackling of energy and a shower of sparks, a sudden roar of agony from the Monster. It fell back and prowled angrily around the ship for a moment. Then it launched another attack, only to be repelled in the same way. Roaring angrily it started to retreat, finally disappearing into the jungle.

Vishinsky raised his hand in salute. 'Thank you, Doctor. You appear to have saved all our lives.'

If Salamar felt any gratitude, he soon got over it. 'All right Doctor. Tell us what you know about that— thing out there.'

Ignoring him, the Doctor looked at Sorenson. 'Professor, you're a scientist. Surely you appreciate the dangers of transferring this type of highly-energised material from one dimension to another?'

Sorenson blinked at him. 'But to effect such a transfer was the entire purpose of my expedition.'

'You're tampering with incredibly dangerous forces.'

'The energy-creature's gone now.'

'For the moment. But while those mineral samples are on board I assure you it will always come back.'

Vishinsky cut in. 'Are you saying we can't take off?'

The Doctor groaned. Wouldn't they *ever* get it into their heads? 'Not until you abandon those mineral samples.'

The idea of losing his samples threw Sorenson into a panic. 'But we can't do that! We need those samples. The fate of the entire Morestran civilisation depends on them.'

'Why?'

'Our sun is dying, Doctor. By taking material from this planet we can re-fuel it, and save our civilisation.'

'I understand your problem, Professor, and I sympathise. But believe me, interfering with Zeta Minor isn't the answer. You'll only bring about a far worse cataclysm, involving many more civilisations than your own. You must find an alternative energy-source.'

Salamar was back in his command chair. 'Let me get this clear, Doctor. You say that if we jettison the canisters we shall be able to take off?'

'I think so. Provided you make it quite clear that your intention is to depart as you came—empty-handed!'

Vishinsky said cynically, 'And just how do we communicate this intention? Is someone going to go and talk to that thing out there.'

'I am,' replied the Doctor calmly. 'I'm not without influence. But it will take a little time.'

'Very well,' said Salamar. 'But the girl will stay here as hostage ... Just in case. You may go, Doctor.'

The Doctor made for the door. As he passed Sarah she reached out to stop him. 'Doctor, please don't ...'

'I must, Sarah.'

'Then let me come with you.'

'It wouldn't work. I must go by myself.' Gently he moved her hand away. 'I'll be careful, I promise.' With that he was gone.

A few minutes later Salamar stood at the viewing port and saw the Doctor emerge from the ship and set off through the jungle.

He returned to the console. 'Vishinsky, launch the Oculoid. I want to keep track of the Doctor.'

The Doctor moved through the jungle, making steadily for the Black Pool. He heard the droning sound above, and looked up to see the Oculoid Tracker hovering over him. The Doctor grinned wryly and went on his way.

He reached the Black Pool at last. Near its edge he found the withered body of Ponti. The Doctor examined it a moment and then stood up. The alien entity had rejected this body as it had the others. Did it know that its touch meant death to creatures from this dimension? Did it know it was killing them, and did it care? Did it think at all, as we know thought? There was only one way to find out.

The Doctor stood on the very edge of the Black Pool. He concentrated his mind and sent the impulses of his thoughts deep into its depths.

He heard a kind of crackling, faint at first, then steadily louder. There was a swirl of dust about his feet, the shimmering of a red outline in the air. The

Doctor felt the immense alien force bearing down on him. 'No, you don't understand,' he called. 'I'm not your enemy. I want to help ... to help ...' The Doctor backed away ...

Sarah stood watching the scene on the Oculoid scanner. They had followed the Doctor's journey through the jungle. They'd watched him find the body, and seen him stand waiting.

Now they saw him stumble, lose his balance and fall backwards into the Black Pool.

Silently it swallowed him up.

7

The Creature in the Corridor

Helplessly Sarah watched the Doctor disappear. 'Doctor!' she shouted. Realising she was talking to a monitor screen she ran to Vishinsky. '*Do* something,' she pleaded.

There was real sympathy in Vishinsky's voice. 'I'm sorry. There's nothing to be done.'

Sorenson agreed. 'Your friend has disappeared into the vortex between the universes. At least he'll have a chance to find out if his theories are true.' Dismissing the Doctor's end with his usual scientific detachment, Sorenson looked severely at Salamar. 'Night is coming. We should prepare to launch, Controller.'

'I agree,' said Salamar briskly. 'Vishinsky, see that Professor Sorenson's samples are removed from the ship.'

If Sorenson's attitude to the Doctor's disappearance had been lacking in emotion, the threat to his beloved samples produced a very different reaction. 'You can't leave those canisters behind, Controller.'

(The arguments began afresh, and in the middle of the wrangling Sarah slipped silently away.)

'Those minerals are endangering the safety of my ship,' insisted Salamar. 'They must and will be jettisoned.'

Sorenson was almost crying with rage. 'You arrogant young fool! The whole purpose of your ship, your command, is to get me and that material back to the home planet.'

'So you can be hailed as the saviour of the Morestran race?' sneered Salamar. 'Oh no, Professor. My orders were to find your party and get back.'

'But if you abandon that material you will destroy my work. You'd have done better to leave me on the planet to die.'

Salamar wearied of the discussion. 'Professor Sorenson, I must remind you that you are a civilian passenger on a military vessel. If there is any further argument, I shall place you under arrest.'

It seemed for a moment as if Sorenson would persist. Then, apparently accepting defeat, he turned and strode from the Command Area.

With frantic speed, Sarah forced her way through the jungle. She had no very clear idea of what she was going to do. But she was incapable of accepting the Doctor's death as a distant event on a monitor screen. She *had* to see the place for herself. And if by some remote chance the Doctor had survived, she would be there to help him . . .

The Doctor floated slowly in a dream-like limbo of nothingness. He drifted through many coloured swirling currents, down, down, down . . . It would have been pleasant simply to relax, to float on and on … But a sense of mission began to stir in the Doctor's mind. He had come here for a purpose … As if in response to his new mood, his surroundings seemed to grow brighter, and his swimming motions took him not down, but up. He floated to the top of a long shimmering vortex, a kind of whirlpool in reverse. There at the top something was waiting for him. Something huge, powerful, alien, with its flickering outline etched in fiery red …

De Haan and Morelli tucked a heavy metal canister under each arm, and began staggering out of the quarantine chamber towards the spaceship's exit ramp. As they struggled along the corridor De Haan grumbled, 'Carry it in, then carry it out. That's the Space Service motto.'

Morelli did his best to shrug. 'So? They changed their minds.'

'Why couldn't they change their minds before I lugged the stuff on—just for a change?'

'Listen,' said Morelli patiently. 'The Controller wants it carried outside the ship and dumped beyond the take-off force-field, right? So that's what we do—right?'

'Let's get it over then—it's only another fifty yards!' De Haan took a fresh grip on the canisters. 'Half my service I'm flying one way, the other half I'm coming back—why can't they pay me to stay in one place?'

As they disappeared down the corridor a sliding door opened and Sorenson appeared. He watched them until they turned a curve of the corridor and were out of sight. Then he slipped quietly into the quarantine chamber. The last few canisters were still stacked against the wall. Sorenson sorted rapidly through them, found the one he wanted, and carried it quickly from the quarantine area.

Sarah reached the edge of the Black Pool just in time to see a familiar figure climbing painfully over its rocky rim. 'Doctor!' she called delightedly, and ran to help.

The Doctor seemed exhausted by some enormous effort. His movements were slow and laborious, and Sarah did most of the work of getting him over the rim of the pool. Curiously, he wasn't the slightest bit wet.

She heaved him clear at last and he collapsed in a heap. He stared dazedly at her for a moment, and then finally seemed to recognise her. He managed to sit up and give a smile. 'Hullo Sarah!' he said cheerfully— and then fainted dead away.

Sarah shook him frantically. 'Wake up, Doctor, you must wake up. That spaceship's just about to take off —and the TARDIS is inside!' The Doctor didn't respond. He was completely motionless and scarcely seemed to be breathing. He might almost have been dead.

De Haan came into the control area and saluted Salamar. 'All the canisters are off the ship, sir.'

'Good. We'll prepare for immediate take-off. Vishinsky!'

Once again Vishinsky began the take-off routines. 'Commence preparation. Prepare pre-ignition checks.'

'Pre-ignition checks commenced.'

'Recall Oculoid Tracker.'

Vishinsky glanced at the monitor screen. He stiffened and snapped, 'Cancel last order. Hold all launch preparations.'

Salamar leaned angrily towards him. 'What do you think you're doing?'

'Look at the Oculoid picture, Commander.'

Salamar looked. The picture showed the edge of the Black Pool with Sarah still struggling to revive the Doctor. They saw him stir a little and then relapse into unconsciousness.

Vishinsky turned to Salamar. 'I'm going outside.'

Salamar stared at him. 'Are you taking command?'

'We've got to bring them in.'

'There happen to be higher priorities at the moment than recovering alien corpses, Vishinsky . . .'

'The Doctor's still alive,' said Vishinsky stubbornly. 'I'm going out to get them. Reig, have the sick-bay prepared for when I return.'

'All right, Vishinsky,' said Salamar coldly. 'But remember. We leave this planet before nightfall—with or without you and your alien friends.'

Locked in his cabin, Sorenson was studying the contents of his stolen canister with loving interest. As he

76

watched he dictated notes into a mini-recorder beside him. 'While still on the surface of Zeta Minor, within the stable environment of the spaceship at a maintained pressure of atmosphere, the mineral sample showed a twenty per cent increase in flux activity.' Even as Sorenson spoke, he could see the precious dust changing colour from red to green and then back again.

Sorenson paused for a moment, listening to the low hum of take-off preparations. A wave of dizziness passed over him, and he knuckled his fists into his eyes. He crossed to the mirror and looked at his reflection. The pupils of his eyes had vanished, replaced by flat discs of glaring, luminous red. The effect was indescribably horrible, transforming Sorenson into some strange alien beast.

Sorenson seemed horrified but resigned. It was as if this was not the first time such a horrible transformation had come over him. With shaking hands he produced a glass and a small bottle of black fluid from a locker. The bottle rattled against the glass as he poured a measured dose. The thick black fluid steamed and fizzed inside the glass. Sorenson drained it in one swift gulp, and buried his face in his hands. Then he looked again in the mirror. Slowly the red glare faded from his eyes, and he became human again.

Almost as if nothing had happened, Professor Sorenson went back to his work. 'This energy flux indicates a substantially higher potential than previous theoretical estimates ...'

In its canister the red dust changed from red to green and back again.

The Oculoid Tracker floated out of the jungle and up to the side of the ship. A hatch opened and the Tracker vanished inside, like a squirrel popping into its hole. Minutes later, Vishinsky and De Haan came out of the jungle, carrying the Doctor. Sarah walked anxiously beside them.

In the sick-bay, a few minutes later, Sarah watched anxiously as Vishinsky attached a variety of sinister-looking electronic instruments to the Doctor's body. He frowned at the sight of the readings. 'Electro-function's almost non-existent.'

'But he *is* alive,' said Sarah desperately. 'I've seen him like this before.'

Vishinsky nodded to De Haan, who stood by the controls of the medical unit. 'Raise the stimulation intensity to twelve degrees.'

De Haan looked worried. 'That's way over the safety limits.'

'Do it!'

De Haan obeyed. The Doctor's body gave a convulsive jerk, and his chest began rising and falling as he breathed in laboured gasps.

'You see, he's alive,' said Sarah excitedly.

De Haan began removing the electrodes from the Doctor's body. 'Don't expect too much. They often move under stimulation. It's just a nervous reflex.'

78

'Well, at least he's still breathing,' said Vishinsky.

The Doctor began to stir and mutter. Sarah leaned over him. 'He's coming round.'

A voice blared from a wall speaker. 'Stand by for take-off. Vishinsky to Command Area, De Haan to Engineering.'

Vishinsky made for the door. As he was leaving Sarah said, 'Vishinsky ... thanks for all the help.'

Vishinsky's grim face cracked into an unexpected smile. 'I reckon I owed him something.' He disappeared down the corridor, and De Haan followed.

Take-off preparations were well advanced when Vishinsky entered the Command Area, and his lateness earned him a frown of displeasure from Salamar. 'There you are at last, Vishinsky. Take over, will you?'

Vishinsky slid into place and glanced at Morelli, who was back on duty at the control console. 'Pressurisation complete,' reported Morelli.

'Activate cyclo-stimulators.'

'Power jets hooked in.'

'Prepare for ignition.' Vishinsky looked round the Command Area. 'Well, if we don't make it this time, we never will.'

The Doctor opened his eyes and sat up. 'What's that noise?'

'We're taking off. Doctor, are you sure you're all right?'

He stared wildly at her. 'Those canisters of Sorenson ...'

'Don't worry, they've all been dumped.'

The Doctor sank back with a sigh of relief. 'Thank goodness! I gave my promise as a Time Lord, you see.'

'Your promise as a Time Lord? What happened in that Black Pool?'

The Doctor smiled. 'I'm afraid it's not so easy to explain ...'

'I suppose you just popped into this other universe and had a chat?'

The Doctor thought of all the wonder and terror of his journey into another dimension, of the strangeness of his encounter with a creature so completely and utterly alien. He sought for a word that would sum it all up. 'I ... communicated,' he said softly. 'I even made a sort of bargain. If the Morestrans leave now, taking nothing with them, they will be ... pardoned and released.'

The take-off sound had been drowned by a horrible groaning noise. 'Well, they're *trying* to leave all right,' said Sarah. 'But they seem to be having trouble again!'

The Doctor put his hand in his pocket and produced the ornately decorated little tin. 'Good grief, I'd completely forgotten. Come on, Sarah!'

The Doctor swung his legs from the bed and ran from the room.

To conserve energy for take-off, only the dim working lights were on in the corridor. They didn't see the dark figure lurking at the end of the corridor. It drew back into the darkness, and its eyes glowed a fiery red.

Vishinsky and Salamar leant tensely over a monitor screen. It showed the surface of Zeta Minor receding slowly from beneath them—receding far *too* slowly. Vishinsky shook his head unbelievingly. 'We're not going to make it!'

'Activate secondary boosters,' snapped Salamar.

'Secondary launch boosters activated.'

Morelli looked up from his instruments. 'Gravity pull is *increasing*, sir.'

'I want ten seconds at maximum fuel burn.'

Vishinsky leaned closer. 'That's crazy, Controller. If it doesn't work ...

'You heard me. Ten seconds!'

The drone of the drive-units rose to an agonised howl—and still the planetary surface hung obstinately below them. 'Gravity drag increasing,' reported Morelli. 'Height only thirty miles—and decreasing.' Despite all the engines could do, they were being dragged back to the surface of the planet.

The Doctor and Sarah entered in time to hear this. The Doctor took a swift look at the instrument readings. 'That's not gravity, gentlemen. That's anti-matter.'

Salamar said, 'Impossible. All canisters were unloaded.'

The Doctor produced his little tin. 'Except for this one.'

'What's in there?'

'Anti-matter, I'm afraid,' said the Doctor apologetically. 'How else do you think I survived in the pool? It was a sort of—passport.'

The Controller stared at the tin. 'And there's enough in there to hold this spaceship back?'

'More than enough.'

Salamar snatched the tin from the Doctor's hand. 'You fool! Morelli, get this to the jettison hatch—fast!'

Morelli took the little tin and ran from the Command Area.

They all waited tensely. For a moment nothing happened. The drive-units continued their agonised howling. Then suddenly the invisible chain binding them snapped and the Morestran Probe shot away from Zeta Minor like a stone from a catapult. On the monitor screen the planet dropped away from beneath them.

There was a babble of congratulations, and Vishinsky worked hard restoring the drive-units to normal. Finally he sat back with a grunt of relief. 'That should hold her for a while. At last we're on our way!'

The ship's corridors were in semi-darkness and Morelli had to grope his way along the corridors on his way back from the jettison hatch. He heard a door open nearby, and De Haan's familiar voice, 'Hey, Morelli, when do we get some light down here?'

Morelli grinned in the darkness. Trust De Haan to be the one to complain. 'We had some trouble on take-off, switched all the power to the propulsion systems. Don't worry, it'll soon be sorted out.' He went on down the corridor.

De Haan shouted after him, 'Well, get a move on. Do

they think Command Area's the only place anyone's working?' He went back into the drive section, reappearing a moment later with a heavy flashlight. Just as he switched it on a single terrifying scream echoed down the corridor. It cut off suddenly, and there was utter silence.

De Haan yelled, 'Morelli? Hey, Morelli!'

He heard a distant rustle of movement and swung the torch beam down the corridor. For a moment he caught sight of a face—but not a human face. It was bestial, wolfish and hairy—and the eyes glowed red.

De Haan jumped back, the torch beam wavered, and the thing disappeared in the darkness. By the time he shone the light beam back down the corridor, it had vanished. Cautiously De Haan moved along the corridor, his concern for Morelli struggling with his fear. He shone the light along the floor and spotted a crumpled figure. He ran up to it and gently turned it over. It was Morelli. His entire body had withered into a bloodless husk.

8

Marooned in Space

Although things had improved in the Command Area, they were still a long way from normal. At first the spaceship seemed to be making headway. Then the strange force that was dragging them back to Zeta Minor reasserted itself. Vishinsky checked the instrument readings yet again. 'Height two hundred miles ... we're in free space, but we're still losing speed. And the drag effect is *increasing*. I don't understand it.'

The Doctor leaned over his shoulder. 'Well I do. Search the ship.'

'Why?'

'Because there must still be anti-matter somewhere on board. It's the only explanation.'

Salamar whirled round in his command chair. 'Impossible, Doctor.'

Vishinsky leaned forward. 'Controller, we are using fuel at thirty units over normal. At this rate we'll never reach our own solar system.'

'Does that mean we're marooned in space?' asked Sarah.

The Doctor's reply was far from encouraging. 'Yes —if we're not vaporised first.'

'And just *why* should we be vaporised, Doctor?' asked Salamar.

'Anti-matter,' said the Doctor simply. 'Anti-matter

in collision with matter. It's called radiation annihilation. The stuff that's on this ship won't remain stable much longer. When it goes critical, there'll be a release of energy far more intense than nuclear fission.'

Salamar's voice rose almost to a scream. 'I tell you there is no anti-matter on board this ship!'

'And I tell you there is,' said the Doctor calmly. 'There's *got* to be.'

De Haan rushed into the Command Area. His face was white and he was shaking with fear. 'Controller, Morelli's been killed. There's some kind of animal ... I saw it. It's in sector three ...'

He began a babble of explanations but Vishinsky held up his hand. 'Hold it a moment, De Haan.' He turned to Reig at the console. 'General Alert! I want everyone armed. Now then, De Haan, get a grip on yourself—and tell me exactly what happened.'

A terrifying figure staggered into the little cabin that had been assigned to Professor Sorenson. Its twisted bestial face was covered with shaggy hair—the hands were savage claws and the eyes glowed an uncanny fiery red. It staggered to a locker and clumsily fumbled out a bottle and a glass, pouring the black liquid into the glass. With the glass held clumsily in two clawed hands, it drained every drop of the foaming potion and buried its head in the beast-like paws.

A few minutes later, it raised its head and looked in the mirror. With a flood of relief, Professor Sorenson saw his own human face looking back at him. He held up his hands—they were human hands once again. There was only the faintest hint of a fading red glare in his eyes to remind him of the beast he had become— and might well become again. He flung himself sobbing on to the bunk.

Minutes later, he was aroused by the incessant sound of a buzzer. He flicked the communicator switch. A voice said, 'Professor Sorenson?'

'Yes ... what is it?' His voice sounded strange and feeble in his own ears.

The voice from the communicator said, 'Report at once to sector three, Professor. Controller Salamar wants you—it's an emergency.'

The communicator clicked into silence. Shakily Sorenson rose. He took a last reassuring look in the mirror and then left the cabin.

In the sick-bay the Doctor and Sarah watched Vishinsky carry out a preliminary check on Morelli's body. Sarah tried not to look at the pitiful dried husk. It lay on the shelf-tray so recently occupied by the Doctor, shrouded in plastic sheet. Vishinsky said, 'The pathology read-out is identical to the others. Total dehydration, right down to the bone marrow.'

'Maybe that thing from the planet got on board somehow,' suggested Sarah.

Vishinsky scratched his head. 'I don't see how. The force-field was operating all the time the hatch was open. It cuts in automatically.'

The Doctor stood lost in thought, rubbing his chin.

'I wonder,' he said softly. 'I wonder ...' He took the computer print-out from Vishinsky and started studying it.

Professor Sorenson and Controller Salamar stood conferring in a quiet corner of sector three. All around them armed guards were searching the area, and finding nothing. Others were using detection devices to hunt for traces of anti-matter.

'You're a scientist, Professor Sorenson,' Salamar was saying. 'I'm relying on you to help me. We must stand together. This Doctor fellow's won Vishinsky over—I don't trust either of them. We've got to deal with this matter ourselves. Surely you must have *some* theory?' There was a note of hysteria in Salamar's voice, and he kept glancing round suspiciously as if expecting to be spied on.

Sorenson thought hard. It was clear that the Controller was on the verge of cracking up. But Salamar's irrational state could be very useful in diverting attention from Sorenson's own terrible problems. Slowly he said, 'I agree with you, Controller. All the deaths have been caused by a technology quite alien to us. That would seem to point to the Doctor and his friend ... since they are both aliens.'

Salamar nodded eagerly. Clearly the theory was the one he was most eager to accept. Then a snag struck him. 'But the Doctor and the girl were both in the Command Area when Morelli was killed.'

Sorenson waved aside this little difficulty. 'Some kind

of remote-control device. A booby trap ... that device in the quarantine berth might well contain the answer. There might even be a hidden confederate ...'

Vishinsky flicked the communicator switch. 'Crew records? What denomination was Morelli?'

A few seconds later the voice from the communicator said, 'Morelli was Morestran orthodox.'

Vishinsky touched a button and strange music began drifting from a nearby speaker. He went on with his task, sealing the plastic shroud around Morelli's body with a laser-pencil. He reached out and turned a control so that the music faded to inaudibility.

'We may have to play the last rites, but there's nothing in the regulations about listening to them!'

Sarah looked at him in horror. 'Are you telling me that *this* is Morelli's funeral?'

'Routine disposal procedure.' Vishinsky finished his work and stepped back. He pressed a button and the tray on which Morelli lay slid slowly into the wall.

'Where is it going?'

'Out into space of course.'

'Just to *drift*, for ever and ever?'

Vishinsky raised an eyebrow. 'It's neat and tidy.'

'It's horrible,' said Sarah emphatically.

A hatch opened in the side of the ship, and a shrouded form was ejected with enough force to send it well clear of the ship. Outlined against the background of stars it began drifting slowly away on its endless journey.

Vishinsky checked that the body had been properly ejected, and straightened up. 'Well, that's it. Another good soldier gone to join the biggest army of them all.'

Sarah realised there was real grief behind his flippant manner. She touched his arm. 'I'm sorry.'

Vishinsky smiled wryly at her. 'I'll be glad to get away from this planet. It's cost me a lot of friends.'

Sublimely unaware that he had just been attending a funeral, the Doctor looked up from his print-out. 'Vishinsky, I'd like a complete medical check made on everybody on board.'

'Why?' Vishinsky asked bluntly. 'Seems a funny time for a health programme.'

'Because the more I think about it, the more I'm convinced that someone must have become contaminated. Someone is carrying the anti-matter in the cells of his own body.'

'Is that possible, Doctor?'

'For a time certainly. But there would be the most terrible side-effects. For one thing . . .'

The Doctor was interrupted by the arrival of Salamar and Sorenson, both grim and determined. It was Salamar who spoke. 'Doctor, I insist that you let me examine that machine of yours.' To reinforce his words, he drew the blaster from his holster.

'You want to examine the TARDIS? Whatever for?'

'We believe that *you* are responsible for all the deaths that have occurred. Unless you co-operate fully, I shall kill you and the girl without compunction.'

'Thanks very much,' said Sarah indignantly. '*That's* what you get for trying to help people.'

The Doctor casually waved Salamar's blaster aside. 'What *is* the matter with you, old chap? I thought we'd got over all that nonsense. Surely you realise by now that I'm on your side?'

Vishinsky gave the Doctor his support. 'Remember, Controller, the Doctor risked his life to help us.'

'That was simply a ruse to gain our confidence.'

'Why am I supposed to be doing all this?' asked the Doctor wearily.

It was Sorenson who had the answer to that one. 'There must be many other civilisations, just as desperate for new energy sources as we are. My discoveries on Zeta Minor would be of immense value to any one of them.'

'I'm not so sure,' said the Doctor crushingly. 'Professor Sorenson, has it ever occurred to you that you might be mistaken in your theories?'

The Doctor could scarcely have said anything more calculated to enrage the Professor. 'No, sir, it has not,' shouted Sorenson. 'I have devoted my lifetime to the study of alternative energy and ...'

They were interrupted by an urgent voice from the communicator. 'Command Area here, Controller. We're in trouble. The ship's stopped moving.'

'That's impossible!'

'I say again, Controller, the progress register shows *zero*. We're making no headway.'

'All right. I'm coming up.' Salamar hurried to the door.

The others began to follow him, but Salamar paused, the blaster still in his hand. 'You can come, Doctor.

But the girl stays here, a hostage for your good behaviour. Professor Sorenson, you keep an eye on her.'

Sarah gave him a disgusted look. 'He needn't bother. I'm not going to jump out.'

Salamar, Vishinsky and the Doctor hurried from the sick-bay, and Sarah was left alone with Sorenson. Not that she minded particularly. He seemed a harmless little man.

Sorenson was looking curiously at her. 'Your friend the Doctor ... what is his particular field of science?'

Sarah grinned. 'Just about everything. I'm afraid the Doctor is insufferably brilliant.'

'He implied my theories were wrong,' said Sorenson indignantly. 'Well *he's* wrong. He must be. Antiquarks come in three configurations, you see and ...'

Sorenson began a long rambling speech of explanation and self-justification. Sarah didn't understand a word of it, and threw up her hands. 'All right, Professor, all right, save it for the Doctor. I'm not arguing with you!'

Sorenson didn't seem to hear her. He went on with his rambling speech as if lecturing some invisible student audience. Sarah backed away a little nervously. On second thoughts, she was beginning to feel that the Professor wasn't so harmless after all. From the way he was acting, he was more than a little cracked—and there seemed to be a strange reddish glint in his eyes ...

'We're *stationary*,' muttered Vishinsky incredulously. 'We're just—suspended in space.'

'It's crazy,' said Salamar. 'The thrusters are still on full power, and we're not even moving!'

The Doctor cleared his throat. 'The answer is really very simple, gentlemen. You've come to the end of your piece of elastic.'

'What are you talking about?' snarled Salamar.

'It won't stretch any further. For the moment the forces are poised in equilibrium. However, since the drag will certainly increase, and your drive system is already at full power, very shortly the force will start to pull us back.'

'Nothing can do that. Nothing!'

'Anti-matter can,' said the Doctor simply. 'There's still some on board. This proves it.'

Vishinsky said, 'You mean the ship will be dragged back to Zeta Minor?'

'I'm afraid so ... faster and faster. And there's no way to stop it until we find that anti-matter. Until we hit the surface, of course. We'll stop then all right!'

Salamar thrust his blaster to the Doctor's head. 'You're simply trying to divert my attention from the real cause of the trouble.'

'And what might that be?'

'You, Doctor! You and whatever's in that machine of yours. Somehow it's draining the energy from my ship.'

'You're wrong, Salamar.'

'Am I, Doctor? We'll see. You'll show me that machine now—or I'll kill you where you stand!'

9

Sentenced to Death

Salamar was literally shaking with rage, and his blaster was aimed straight at the Doctor's head. The Doctor realised he was in very real danger. The Controller was on the verge of cracking up, and he was quite capable of killing the Doctor because of his insane suspicions. In a soothing voice the Doctor said, 'Very well, Salamar, if that's the only thing which will satisfy you, I'll take you to see the TARDIS.'

Salamar gave a satisfied nod, feeling things were once more under control. 'Take over, Vishinsky. Shall we go, Doctor?'

Salamar's blaster in his back, the Doctor led the way out of the Command Area.

Sarah listened to Sorenson's voice droning on and on. '... anti-matter can be described as matter composed entirely of anti-particles, so the energy available is hypothetically ...' His voice tailed away to a mumble, and he turned away from Sarah, covering his face with his hands.

'Professor, are you all right?'

'Yes, yes, of course. I'm perfectly ...'

Still keeping his back towards her, his hands covering his face, Sorenson staggered clumsily from the sick-bay and blundered off down the corridor.

Sarah wondered if she ought to follow him—but by now she was feeling very strange herself. She had the sensation that something was drawing her mind and soul from her body. In the distance she seemed to hear weird alien sounds ... Suddenly Sarah recognised the sensation. It was exactly the way she'd felt on Zeta Minor when the invisible Monster had passed them in the jungle ...

Sorenson lurched down the darkened corridor, his posture becoming more and more of an animal-like crouch. The hands became claws, and fell away to reveal a bestial wolf-like face in which the eyes glared redly. Snarling hoarsely, the creature that had once been Sorenson prowled along the corridor in search of prey.

De Haan had been assigned to the search of sector three, where he had been scanning corridor walls and floors with a device that was supposed to detect the presence of anti-matter. To his surprise he had picked up the faintest of trails, and with mounting excitement he followed it where it led him—to the corridor outside Sorenson's cabin.

So faint was the trail that De Haan had to back along the corridor on hands and knees so as not to lose it. Shuffling backwards in this fashion he felt himself brush against someone, and the civilian-style shoes and trousers of Professor Sorenson came into view.

'Sorry, Professor,' said De Haan. The reply came not in words but in a low bestial snarl. De Haan glanced up, and his eyes widened in horror. He tried to get to his feet, but the beast was already at his throat. De Haan's dying screams echoed down the metal corridor.

The sounds brought Sarah to her feet. She edged her way to the sick-bay door and stared into the darkness. She could hear a kind of shuffling sound, and dark figures seemed to be struggling. There were hoarse animal-like snarls. Reluctantly Sarah started edging her way towards the sounds ...

The Doctor was in the quarantine bay with Salamar, standing beside the TARDIS. 'Your interest in my Space/Time Machine is very flattering,' he was saying, 'but I assure you, the TARDIS has nothing to do with ...'

Salamar gestured with the blaster. 'Shut up and open it.'

The Doctor sighed and reached for the TARDIS key. He waved towards the TARDIS rather like a tour guide in a museum. 'Now as you see, externally the TARDIS resembles an old-fashioned London Police Box of the ...'

'*I said open it!*'

The Doctor was about to take the key from around his neck when he heard a distant scream. Instinctively, Salamar glanced towards the source of the noise. The Doctor tapped him neatly under the chin, dodged the falling body and ran from the chamber.

Sarah edged slowly towards the end of the corridor. She couldn't see what was happening round the corner, but there was a working light burning at the junction, and she could see shadows reflected on the corridor's end wall. A hunched, ape-like figure crouched over a limp motionless shape, and there was a low growling sound, that seemed to hold a note of triumph. Then came a shuffling, and the hideous growling seemed to move away. When all was silent, Sarah crept cautiously to the corner and peered around. There was a crumpled shape on the floor—the withered, mummified body of De Haan.

Footsteps were pounding along the corridor and the Doctor came to a breathless halt beside her. 'Sarah—what happened?'

'I don't know. I didn't really see it properly. There was a sort of animal ...'

'Anti-man,' said the Doctor gravely. 'It's what I feared all along.'

'Anti-man?'

'A sort of hybrid ... a human being contaminated with anti-matter. There could be a kind of genetic regression, you see, a reversal to the Neanderthal ...'

Before the Doctor could explain further, there came the sound of running footsteps and suddenly there were people running towards them. Salamar was in the lead, with Vishinsky and some armed guards close behind. He looked down at the pathetic shape on the floor and then raised his blaster. 'That's De Haan. You've killed De Haan!'

'Don't be a fool, Salamar,' said the Doctor impatiently. 'I was with *you* when we heard him scream.'

Salamar was beyond reason. He raised his blaster, and aimed it at the Doctor's head, the intention to kill plain in his distorted face. Sarah screamed, 'No!' and flung herself towards him, knocking up his arm just as he fired. The blaster-bolt grazed the side of the Doctor's head and he reeled and fell. Salamar raised his blaster to fire again, but Vishinsky caught his arm and wrenched it aside. 'No, Controller!'

Salamar stared wildly at him. 'Don't you see, Vishinsky. They've killed De Haan.'

'*Something* killed De Haan. We don't know that it was them.'

'Of course it was them,' said Salamar feverishly. He clutched Vishinsky's arm. 'We've got to get rid of them, get them off the ship before they kill us all.' He turned to the guards. 'Take them to the sick-bay!'

The creature in Sorenson's cabin stared horrified into the mirror. It had already swallowed one of the healing draughts, yet the reversion to human form was not complete. The blurred features of Sorenson stared desperately from beneath the face of the beast. Clumsily the creature poured a second dose from the black bottle and swallowed that too. The reversion began again, and soon Sorenson, fully human once more, was staring at his own face in the mirror.

He turned away with a sob of relief, and caught the black bottle with his elbow. Still uncapped, it rolled

97

away under the bunk. Sorenson scrabbled desperately for it, but by the time he recovered it, the bottle was already empty.

Suddenly a familiar, horrible sensation swept over him, and with a gasp of horror he ran back to the mirror. The red glare was already returning to his eyes ...

It was back on Zeta Minor that Sorenson had first noticed the effects of working with anti-matter, the biological reversion that was slowly turning him into a ravening beast. He had prepared the black potion to hold the effect in check, so that he could still go on with his work. But recently the serum had begun to lose its effect, and since his return to the spaceship the pull of the reversion had grown ever stronger. And now the last of the serum was gone. Sorenson had hoped to synthesise a new and stronger serum in the ship's medical section. But now the change was beginning again ... Before he could devise his cure, he might be locked in the form of the beast—for ever.

Sarah had gone quite willingly to the sick-bay, assuming that despite Salamar's wild threats the Doctor would be given some kind of medical care. When they arrived Salamar operated controls in the console and two of the bunk-sized trays that served as beds slid out of the walls. The unconscious Doctor was lifted on to one of them and strapped down. 'Her too,' snapped Salamar, and struggling wildly Sarah was strapped to the other.

'What do you think you're doing?' she yelled. 'I'm not the one who's ill.'

When she was firmly bound, Salamar dismissed the guards and stood staring down at her. His face was quite mad. 'You're familiar with the operation of the ejector trays—you've seen them used on one of your victims. When I press this button you will both slide into the ejector tubes, which will expel you into space.'

Sarah said unbelievingly, 'You can't do that—it's murder. Tell him, Vishinsky.'

'She's right, Controller. We've no real evidence.'

'How much evidence do you want, Vishinsky? The whole crew dead? Eject them. That's an order.'

Vishinsky didn't move. Salamar shoved him aside and stabbed at the button. Slowly the trays bearing the Doctor and Sarah began to retract into the wall of the spaceship.

10

The Monster Runs Amok

Crewman Reig, junior and most inexperienced of the Morestran's flight crew, was hunched nervously over the controls, desperately wishing that the Controller, or better still the imperturbable Vishinsky, would return to the Command Area.

He touched the intercom button and spoke to the engineers in the drive section. 'Maintain boosters at full thrust. We're only just holding. We mustn't get pulled into reverse ...'

A shadow fell over him and he looked up in relief. 'Controller, the drag effect is——' His words ended in a gasp, as he saw the horrifying bestial figure that loomed above him. Terrified, he jabbed the emergency communication button. 'This is Command Deck. Please send help ...'

When the call was heard in the sick-bay, the Doctor and Sarah had almost disappeared into the wall. Only their heads were still projecting.

Vishinsky flicked the intercom. 'Reig? What's happening up there?'

A terrible choking cry came from the speaker. Then silence. Salamar was already running from the room and Vishinsky was about to follow. Desperately Sarah screamed, 'Vishinsky!'

Almost casually, Vishinsky reached out and pressed a button, then turned and ran after Salamar. The ejector trays stopped their remorseless withdrawal, and started to slide back out again.

The Doctor opened one eye and looked muzzily at Sarah. 'This is no moment to be lazing about,' he said severely. 'Isn't it time we were getting up?'

Vishinsky lifted Reig's body from the console. The pitiful withered husk was almost weightless. He laid it gently on the floor. 'If we hadn't been wasting time with your execution, Salamar——'

'It's their fault, they caused it all.'

'Strapped to ejector-trays with both of us standing over them?'

Vishinsky turned back to the console. 'Stand-by crewman to replace Reig on Command Deck. All other crewmen report to assembly points. Red Alert!'

Furiously Salamar shouted, 'Countermand that, Vishinsky. Only the Controller can order Red Alert.'

'I'm replacing you, Salamar. You're not longer fit to hold command. Stay out of my way or I'll have you locked up.'

Salamar stared furiously at the older man. He would have liked to seize control again, to have Vishinsky arrested, but his nerve failed him. Sulkily he muttered, 'All right, Vishinsky. But you'll regret this.'

Ignoring him, Vishinsky turned away and began issuing a stream of orders into the intercom. The ship became alive with the alarm sirens and the sound of running feet.

With the trays fully extended, Sarah was able to wriggle her arms free from the restraining straps. She unbuckled herself and set about freeing the Doctor, who still didn't seem to realise how nearly he'd come to going for a space-walk without a space-suit.

He sat up, listening to the alarms sounding all over the ship. 'What's going on? Where are Salamar and Vishinsky?'

'I think there's been another killing. Doctor, it *is* that thing from the planet. I felt it.'

'You did what?'

'Just before De Haan was killed. I felt this sort of . . . mental suction . . . like when we were in the jungle.'

The Doctor frowned. 'Before De Haan was killed? Was anyone with you?'

Sarah put her hand to her mouth. 'Yes . . . Professor Sorenson!'

The Doctor nodded. 'I was afraid so. He was the logical candidate. The sole survivor of the expedition . . . the anti-man. He's the one who's been affected by anti-matter. His body-cells are being destroyed. It's as if he's regressed back through the scale of human evolution.'

The Doctor rose and went to the door. 'Sarah, go to the Command Deck and tell them to shut off all the interior hatchways. Our only chance is to keep Sorenson isolated.'

'What about you?'

The Doctor was already on his way. 'Sarah, just do as I say!' He vanished down the corridor.

Too experienced to rely on the Red Alert alone, Vishinsky was calling up every department of the ship in turn, issuing clear instructions and making sure that everyone understood the nature of the emergency. Under the influence of his familiar voice, a kind of calm returned to the ship. He checked his list. There was only one more call to make. 'Command Area to Solarium. Who's in charge there?'

The voice that replied still held a faint trace of the lilt of English-speaking Indians on faraway Earth. 'Senior Crewleader Ranjit, sir.'

'Good. You know why we're on Red Alert?'

The voice was uncertain. 'Not exactly, sir. They are saying we picked up some contagion back on the planet.'

'We picked up something else—some animal. It's killed Morelli, De Haan and Reig, so don't take any chances. Keep your men alert, and await further orders.'

'Right, sir.'

Vishinsky sat back in the command chair and considered what to do next. He became aware of Salamar beside him.

Salamar's face twisted into a sneer. 'Well, Vishinsky, what are you going to do now? Why don't you take a look at the course monitor—*Controller*.'

Vishinsky looked, and drew in his breath in horror. 'We're being pulled back—towards Zeta Minor.'

'Come on then,' jeered Salamar, his voice rising. 'You've taken charge. Think up an order that will stop us crashing—because if you don't we're all going to die.'

'It would help if you'd try to keep your nerve, Salamar . . .' Vishinsky turned as Sarah ran panting into the Command Area. 'Where's the Doctor?' he said.

'Don't know,' she gasped. 'He says you're to close all the internal hatches.'

'I'm going to, as soon as I've completed the crew check. Professor Sorenson still hasn't reported in.'

'You mustn't wait for him. He's the one who's behind it all. Do it now! You've got to cut him off.'

'Sorenson's behind it?' said Salamar unbelievingly. 'That's insane.'

'Something on the planet affected him,' explained Sarah impatiently. 'After all, he was there the longest. Vishinsky, please, you've got to close those hatches.'

Salamar pushed her aside. 'Don't listen, Vishinsky. It's another of their tricks.'

'If we'd listened to the Doctor a lot earlier, things might be in a better state.' He turned to the duty crewman. 'Close all section hatchways.'

Obediently the crewman began pressing a row of controls.

All over the Probe steel barriers clanged shut, sealing off section after section of the ship. Standing outside Sorenson's cabin, the Doctor heard the sounds and nodded in satisfaction. He took out his sonic screwdriver, neatly picked the lock of Sorenson's cabin door and slipped inside.

Once inside the small bare cabin the Doctor began a rapid search. He soon turned up the one remaining canister, and found the empty black bottle on the floor.

The Doctor sniffed the bottle cautiously, and tipped out a minute quantity of the glowing red dust on to the table. He shook the last few drops of the liquid on to the powder, which immediately went grey and inert. The Doctor sighed. The whole story was there. Sorenson's infection by the anti-matter, his attempts to find a cure, his eventual, inevitable failure. The Doctor didn't see the door behind him begin to slide open. Then he swung round as someone entered the room.

It was Sorenson. Weary, wild-eyed, dishevelled—but fortunately once more his human self. But for how long, thought the Doctor. He tried to remember the few rare cases of anti-matter infection on the Time Lords' files. Each metamorphosis was followed by a return to the original shape. But the changes came ever more quickly, and the final change was permanent.

As Sorenson advanced upon him the Doctor grabbed the anti-matter canister and held it up like a shield. 'Keep back,' he ordered, and watched Sorenson narrowly. If the Doctor was correct, by this stage in the infection, the presence of a concentration of anti-matter should cause extreme discomfort. Sure enough Sorenson came to a halt, and backed away blinking.

He looked around the room, and seeing the evidence of the Doctor's search, made a pathetic attempt to regain his dignity.

'Doctor, I require an explanation.'

Compassionately the Doctor said, 'I'm sorry, Professor Sorenson, but you are ill.'

'Ill? What do you mean, ill?'

The Doctor lifted the little black bottle. 'When you became infected on Zeta Minor, you tried to develop an oral vaccine to counter the effects of anti-quark penetration. But you didn't succeed.'

'Nonsense. The vaccine worked,' said Sorenson defensively.

'It worked for a time. But a cycle of chemical changes has been set up. There's no way back, Professor.'

Sorenson's defences crumpled. He groaned and collapsed on the bunk. Sadly the Doctor said, 'Your tissues are now so monstrously hybridised that the next metabolic change will be the final one.'

Sorenson stumbled to his feet and stared searchingly at his face in the mirror.

The Doctor's voice was gentle but remorseless. 'There is now only one way to save the lives of everyone on this ship. The remaining sources of anti-matter must be jettisoned. That means this canister, Professor—and you, yourself. There isn't much time. The sick-bay is in this section, you'll be able to reach it in a couple of minutes ...'

Sorenson groaned, 'No ... no ...'

The Doctor said sadly, 'You and I are scientists, Professor. We buy our privilege to experiment only at the cost of responsibility. *Total* responsibility.'

Sorenson stood up. He took a deep breath and then

said, 'You're right, of course, Doctor. The fault was mine. My hypothesis was false. Now I must pay the price.'

He turned and walked slowly from the room. The Doctor stood very still, the anti-matter container in his hand. Sorenson turned down the corridor to the sick-bay—and the ejection shutes.

'Look it's no use going on at *me*,' said Sarah vigorously. 'You'll have to ask the Doctor when he gets here. All I know is, he say the anti-matter has turned Professor Sorenson into some kind of monster.'

Salamar had been listening with keen interest. 'So if we jettison the remaining anti-matter *and* destroy Sorenson, the trouble will be over?'

'I suppose so, though I don't know how you can . . .'

'I do!' Salamar went to a locked wall-case, smashed it open with the handle of his blaster and removed a stubby metal cylinder from a rack inside.

Vishinsky leapt up. 'Don't be a fool, Salamar.'

Salamar had the cylinder free by now. Tucking it under his arm he covered Vishinsky with his blaster. 'Keep back!'

Vishinsky backed away.

'What's he got there?' whispered Sarah.

'One of the spare neutron accelerators. Take off the shield and it emits a stream of radioactive particles . . .' Sarah saw there was a heavy lead cap on one end of the cylinder, and controls set into the other.

Salamar was moving towards the door, now barred

by the metal hatch. 'All right, Vishinsky, open the hatch.'

Vishinsky kept his voice calm and reasonable. 'Salamar, if you take the shielding off that neutron accelerator you'll be dead in minutes.'

'Maybe so. But I'll take Sorenson with me. I'm going to save your life, Vishinsky, all your lives. What's the matter with you all, don't you want to live?'

Vishinsky shook his head. 'You're out of your mind.'

'Oh no! This is leadership. Strong action. It's why *I'm* Controller. Open the hatch!'

The duty crewman made a sudden dive for the cylinder. Salamar jumped back and blasted him down. He levelled the blaster at Vishinsky. 'Now—*open* that hatch! Or do I have to shoot you and open it myself?'

Still Vishinsky didn't move. Sarah touched his arm. 'Let him go, Vishinsky. No use getting yourself killed for nothing.'

Vishinsky touched a control and the hatch slid open. Salamar paused in the doorway, an insanely triumphant smile on his face. 'You Controller? You haven't a hope, Vishinsky!' He disappeared through the door.

Vishinsky shrugged and closed the hatch behind him. 'Well, if the radiation doesn't get him, Sorenson will.'

Sorenson walked slowly along the corridor towards the sick-bay. Gradually his posture became more hunched, his step more dragging. He could feel the terrible change coming over him once more. With the last vestiges of his human will, he forced himself to stagger on.

By the time he entered the sick-bay, the change was well under way. The creature that was half-Sorenson, half-beast, collapsed on to one of the ejector trays. A hand reached out for the ejection button—then changed slowly into a claw. The form and personality of Sorenson were totally submerged in the beast—and the beast was determined to survive. The claw drew back, and the creature sprang from the tray and lurched away down the corridor.

Salamar moved along the corridor exalted by his insane sense of purpose. He paused at a junction and touched the control that activated the neutron accelerator. Immediaely the cylinder began to pulse with light. With the all-powerful weapon in his hands, Salamar felt like a superman. The fact that the deadly radiation was already seeping through his own body didn't bother him in the least. Levelling the accelerator like a rifle, he strode on his way.

He turned a corner and saw a metal shutter barring his path. Salamar smiled cunningly. Even here he had managed to outwit Vishinsky. Pulling a key from beneath his tunic, he opened the shutter and continued on his way.

For what seemed like a very long time the Doctor sat sadly on Sorenson's bunk, the anti-matter cylinder in his hands. Then he rose. It was time to get rid of the cylinder through one of the smaller disposal chutes—and to check whether Sorenson had carried through his act of self-sacrifice. The Doctor made his way to the sick-bay and went inside. He saw that the ejector trays were still open—and there was no sign of Sorenson. He flicked the switch on the intercom. 'Command Area? This is the Doctor. How are things up there?'

Vishinsky's voice was strained. 'Bad, Doctor. We're still accelerating towards Zeta Minor. Have you located the anti-matter?'

'Some of it. But there's another source—Sorenson himself.'

He heard Sarah's voice. 'Doctor, Salamar's gone off his head. He's out hunting Sorenson now ...'

Then Vishinsky again, 'He's carrying a neutron accelerator. He plans to use it to kill Sorenson.'

The Doctor was appalled. 'What? He's got to be stopped! If he exposes the anti-matter creature to neutron radiation——' He broke off. 'How long till we hit the planet?'

'About twenty minutes.'

'Open the hatches, Vishinsky. I've got to find them before it's too late!' The Doctor raced from the sick-bay and along the corridors, the clang of opening shutters sounding all around him.

Salamar too was racing through the ship with the speed and strength of madness. After a long and fruitless search he found himself outside the quarantine bay.

He paused, a cunning smile on his face. Of course ... the very place. He crept quietly inside.

At first he could see nothing in the gloomy, unlit chamber. Nothing except the TARDIS looming dark against one wall. Then, from somewhere behind it, he heard low hoarse breathing.

Triumphantly Salamar stepped out into the centre of the chamber, the eerily glowing cylinder held in front of him. 'I know you're there, Sorenson,' he screamed. 'Come out and face me!'

The hoarse breathing turned into a savage growl and the beast lurched out of hiding, eyes glowing red. It let out a savage howl of rage and triumph and advanced on Salamar.

11

An Army of Monsters

Racing along the corridors, the Doctor heard the savage roaring, and sped towards the quarantine bay. As he neared the door the sounds grew louder. 'Salamar, are you in there?' he shouted. 'Whatever you do, don't irradiate that thing. Salamar, can you hear me?'

Salamar heard the Doctor's voice and hesitated for a moment. Then the beast lunged towards him, and instinctively he sprang the clips that held the lead nozzle in place. The nozzle-shield sprang back and a stream of brilliant white light shot out of the accelerator, catching the beast full in the chest. It roared and staggered, then leapt forward once more, grappling with Salamar, absorbing the life force from his body. Salamar gave a terrible scream and died. The beast flung the withered body aside and stood reeling for a moment. It's own body glowed brightly with the force of the radiation it had absorbed. The glow became brighter. It staggered towards the door on the far side of the chamber.

Seconds later the Doctor rushed into the quarantine bay. He saw only Salamar's body, and the still-glowing cylinder at his feet, sending out its deadly beam. Kneeling behind the cylinder, he used the inset controls to de-activate it. The glow faded and the Doctor clipped the lead nozzle back in place. He went over to the intercom.

Sarah and Vishinsky both jumped at the sound of the Doctor's voice. 'I was too late, Salamar's already dead. He's used the neutron accelerator too—if he actually hit Sorenson the effect could be disastrous.'

'You mean things could actually get worse?' said Sarah. 'I don't believe it.'

The Doctor's voice came again. 'Keep the hatches open, and tell the crew to barricade themselves in their own sections. I'll be up as soon as I can.'

The Doctor made a quick check of the quarantine bay, then satisfied that the Sorenson monster had indeed moved on, he set off back towards the Command Deck. The spaceship corridors were strangely silent. Following Vishinsky's orders the spaceship's crew were all locked in their own sections, awaiting further orders.

The Doctor turned a corner and the beast stood facing him. But *not* the horribly real creature into which Sorenson had changed. This was an anti-matter monster, little more than a glowing red outline of the beast which Sorenson had become. Yet the Doctor knew it was just as deadly. As deadly as the giant anti-matter Monster they'd battled with on Zeta Minor.

As the red-outlined beast sprang towards him, the Doctor raised the canister of anti-matter. As with Sorenson himself, it acted as a kind of shield, and the beast retreated roaring. The Doctor edged his way past—only to find another identical beast appearing before him. One in front and one behind, the twin anti-matter beasts closed in on him. The Doctor swung the canister in a menacing arc, dodged round the second monster and backed away down the corridor.

'Why's he taking so *long*,' demanded Sarah worriedly.

Vishinsky shrugged. 'I'll try the quarantine area. He may still be in there.' He leaned forward. 'Doctor, are you there? If you can hear me please identify your position.'

Silence.

Sarah looked at Vishinsky. 'I know something's happened to him.' She leaned forward over the mike. 'Doctor, are you there? Are you all right?'

There came a sudden hammering at the hatchway sealing off the Command Area. Vishinsky opened it and the Doctor fell inside.

'Close all hatchways,' he gasped. 'That will hold them for a while.'

'*Them?*' asked Sarah. She had a sudden suspicion that things really *had* got worse.

'Them!' confirmed the Doctor. 'The monster has multiplied!'

In a nearby corridor, one of the anti-matter beasts found its way blocked by the steel shutter. It advanced steadily till its glowing shape was outlined against the hatch. Then it passed through the hatch and continued on its way. To creatures from the universe of anti-matter, the strongest metal was no barrier.

The Doctor, Sarah and Vishinsky watched the scene on a monitor. They saw a whole series of the anti-matter creatures burn their way through the heavy metal barriers. 'They just walk right through,' said Sarah wonderingly.

Vishinsky mopped his forehead. 'Doctor, what *are* those things?'

'Anti-matter duplicates,' said the Doctor solemnly. 'Copies of Sorenson—or rather of the thing that he turned into. Pure anti-matter. The neutron accelerator simply boosted the Sorenson monster's power—and it split off and multiplied.'

'So how many of these things are there?' asked Vishinsky despairingly.

'As many as the Sorenson monster wants there to be. We could be facing a whole army of them.'

'They were moving towards the Solarium Chamber,' muttered Vishinsky. 'I'd better warn the crew.' He flicked a switch and a confused babble of voices filled the air. 'Ranjit, are you there? What's happening?'

'They're attacking, coming right through the walls. Help us ...' There were more shouts, more screams and then a terrible silence.

'Seven men gone,' said Vishinsky grimly. 'And sixteen minutes before we hit the planet.'

Sarah looked up at the Doctor, who stood brooding over the console. 'Doctor—how can we stop them?'

For a moment he didn't answer her, his eyes far away. Then he straightened up. 'Open the hatches, Vishinsky. Give me time to reach the quarantine bay, then close them again.' Picking up the canister of anti-matter, the Doctor made for the door. 'You'd better stay here with Vishinsky, Sarah, I may be some time.'

Sarah said nothing, but tears filled her eyes as she watched him go.

Vishinsky said grimly. 'Whatever he plans to do, he'd better be quick. We've got just under fifteen minutes before we hit Zeta Minor.'

The Doctor met only one of the anti-matter beasts as he made his way along the corridors, and it retreated snarling when he raised the canister. He had the feeling that no serious attempt was being made to stop him. His adversary was waiting for him elsewhere.

When he stepped into the darkened quarantine bay, he knew he was right. He heard a hoarse animal-like breathing. The living beast, the original Sorenson monster, had returned and was awaiting him.

Canister in one hand, blaster in the other, the Doctor advanced towards the sound. An anti-matter beast sprang up in front of him and he used the canister to drive it back. Another appeared and then another. Whichever way the Doctor moved one of the glowing outlines sprang up before him. The hoarse breathing of the lurking beast changed into a hyena-like cackle of mirth.

The Doctor found that the ring of anti-matter

monsters was herding him towards the sound. Their roars reached a triumphant crescendo. He heard hoarse breathing from behind him, spun round and saw the real beast looming above him. He raised the blaster and fired, and the beast staggered back against the TARDIS. Discarding the blaster the Doctor whipped the key from around his neck and opened the door. The beast tumbled inside and the Doctor followed, closing the door behind him.

The roaring of the anti-matter monsters was suddenly cut off. The Doctor knew that inside the TARDIS he was safe from their attack. But he still had the original beast to deal with. It lay slumped by the wall of the TARDIS, breathing hoarsely.

The Doctor fished in a seldom-used locker and dragged out a set of heavy chains, a relic of some long-ago adventure. He used them to bind the monster hand and foot, then hurried to the TARDIS control console and set co-ordinates for Zeta Minor.

There was a wheezing, groaning sound in the quarantine bay and the TARDIS faded from sight. The ring of anti-matter beasts surrounding it howled with baffled rage.

Inside the TARDIS, the beast recovered to find itself securely bound. It roared with insane rage, and began flinging itself to and fro in a frantic effort to break its bonds. Busy at the controls, the Doctor ignored it. Curiously enough it was the relative shortness of the journey that was worrying him. The TARDIS wasn't really built for short hops and it was easier to reach a distant galaxy than a planet just a few hundred miles away. Moreover, accuracy was of supreme importance. His arrival point had to be very precisely judged. Busy with his calculations, the Doctor failed to notice that the beast had already wrenched one arm free from its bonds ...

The closeness of Zeta Minor was also worrying Vishinsky, though for very different reasons. He studied the instrument readings and looked grimly at Sarah. 'Acceleration seventy-three STS.'

Sarah looked blank. 'What does that mean?'

'It means we smash into Zeta Minor in exactly eight minutes—if those creatures don't get to us first.'

Vishinsky had closed the shutters again according to the Doctor's instructions, and the Command Area was once more ringed with steel doors. It took the anti-matter creatures only a minute or two to burn through them, but even the smallest delay was valuable.

The anti-matter monsters continued to advance. One by one they passed through the heavy metal shutters. Worriedly Vishinsky studied the illuminated chart of the ship. 'They seem to be all around us. And they're getting closer.' He checked the instruments. 'Six minutes to go. Come on, Sarah, I'll need your help.' He opened a small door at the other end of the Command Area.

Sarah got up. 'Where are we going?'

'To get the force-field equipment. If we can lay a force-field around the Command Area we may be able to hold them off.'

Sarah followed him to the little door. 'Six, no five minutes till we crash, and you want to set up a force-field?'

Vishinsky looked at her in surprise. 'Sure. What do you want us to do—give up?'

He led her along a short corridor to a heavy metal door marked 'FORCE-FIELD EQUIPMENT—DANGER'. Unlocking the door Vishinsky plunged inside, emerging moments later with a jumble of electronic equipment. It included a couple of things like miniature radar scanners, linked by a tangle of other equipment. He began piling the lot into Sarah's arms. 'Here, you take this and I'll bring the control box.' It was all quite mad, thought Sarah, as he loaded her up. But then, they might as well go down fighting. Vishinsky dashed back into the force-field store and emerged staggering under the weight of a heavy black metal box with controls set into the top.

Suddenly Sarah pointed. 'Look!' Not just one, but a whole line of anti-matter beasts was marching along the corridor towards them. Sarah remembered the Doctor's words, 'an army of monsters'.

Weighed down by the heavy equipment, Sarah and Vishinsky retreated as fast as they could. The leading monster was almost upon them when Vishinsky shoved Sarah into the Command Area and slammed the door in its face.

Quickly Vishinsky started assembling the equipment. 'It's directional, you see. We can seal off the entire Command Area.'

Sarah looked at him in wonder as he worked frantically on the equipment. She remembered his earlier estimate—six minutes until impact. It must have taken at least half that to get the equipment. They would all die anyway in a minute or so. Yet here was Vishinsky straining every muscle to gain them a minute or two's immunity from the anti-matter monster's attack. It was either heroic or crazy, thought Sarah. Or maybe it was both.

She saw a glowing outline appear on the door they'd just come through, and pointed. 'Look!' The first of the anti-matter monsters was burning its way through the door.

Just as the TARDIS landed, the beast managed to break free. The Doctor saw the movement from the corner of his eye, touched the TARDIS door-controls, grabbed the anti-matter canister and sprang out of the still-opening door just as the beast lunged towards him. It missed its grip by inches, and roaring with rage, pursued him from the TARDIS.

As the Doctor flew through the doors he gave himself a quick mental pat on the back. The TARDIS had arrived, just as he'd planned, right beside the Black Pool. 'Pretty good piece of navigation that.' thought the Doctor, and hurled himself forward to escape the beast's next lunge. Slowly the Doctor backed away and the beast stalked him along the edge of the pool, growling ferociously. A length of heavy chain still clanked round its neck, like an improvised collar.

The beast charged again, and the Doctor dodged back, luring it to the very brink of the pool. Then suddenly the Doctor sprang forward, caught the dangling length of chain, swung the beast round on the end of it, like a man throwing the hammer, and just as suddenly let go. Spun off-balance, the beast reeled backwards and tripped. With a terrifying howl it plunged into the depths of the Black Pool. So savage had been the Doctor's final heave that he lost his balance too, and nearly tumbled in after it, saving himself at the last minute by grabbing a projecting rock. He hung above the black depths for a moment, then pulled himself to safety. The Doctor stood, chest heaving, drawing deep agonised breaths. He hunted round until he found the anti-matter canister, dropped in the struggle, and tossed it into the very centre of the pool.

Vishinsky abandoned his work on the force-field as the anti-matter beast burned its way through the door. It was followed by another, and another, and still another. The line seemed endless. Vishinsky grabbed Sarah's hand and pulled her behind the flimsy shelter of the console. The encircling ring of monstrous shapes came closer and closer. There was nothing they could do now but wait for the inevitable end. Sarah gave Vishinsky's hand a consoling squeeze, and felt the pressure returned. She wondered if the Doctor had survived, if he would return and find their bodies . . .

The nearest monster leaped for them—and vanished. The others vanished in the same instant. They were alone in the Command Area.

Vishinsky stood stunned for a moment. Then his trained reflexes took over and he sprang to the control console. 'Thirty seconds to impact,' he shouted. 'But we're slowing down ... twenty-five seconds.' A sudden tremendous jolt sent them to the floor. Vishinsky picked himself up and scrambled to the console. 'We've stopped. We're still on full power but we've stopped ...'

There was a second, less violent jolt. 'We're moving again,' gasped Sarah, as she picked herself up.

Vishinsky was leaning over the console, his face one enormous grin. 'That's right! We're gaining height. We're moving away from the planet again. *We've done it!*'

For a moment Sarah returned his smile. Then her face became serious again. '*We're* safe. But where's the Doctor?'

The Doctor stood gazing into the depths of the Black Pool. For some reason he felt a strange reluctance to leave. It was as though there was something still unfinished.

The pool seemed to heave and bubble, and to the Doctor's astonishment Sorenson crawled from its depths and collapsed gasping at the edge. Cautiously the Doctor approached him. It was Sorenson all right, apparently cured, free from the trace of the antimatter infection which had so horribly transformed him. The Doctor heaved him to his feet and dragged him inside the TARDIS. The door closed behind them.

Suddenly there came a strange alien crackling from the Black Pool. Outlined in glowing red, an enormous dragon-like shape appeared. It was the Monster of the Black Pool. For a moment it reared above the TARDIS as if to swallow it up. Then it froze, motionless, recognising perhaps that the word of the Time Lord had been kept. Zeta Minor was whole once more.

There was a wheezing, groaning sound and the TARDIS disappeared.

The Monster flowed back into the Black Pool that was its home.

Inside the TARDIS Professor Sorenson gazed around him with an air of total bafflement. 'Where am I? What am I doing here?' Busy at the TARDIS console, the Doctor glanced over his shoulder.

'Professor Sorenson,' he said solemnly, 'you're a very lucky man. You have been released.'

'Released?'

'Because I kept my promise and returned all the anti-matter.'

Sorenson rubbed his eyes dazedly. 'I've been having the most terrible nightmares. Something about some kind of savage beast ...' He became aware of his surroundings. 'Where am I? This doesn't look a bit like the Morestran Probe Ship.'

'It isn't,' said the Doctor drily. 'Just rest awhile, Professor. Everything's going to be all right now.'

Mentally the Doctor crossed his fingers. This was his second tricky navigational job in swift succession. He now had to put the TARDIS back inside a spaceship which was no doubt zooming away from Zeta Minor just as fast as it could travel.

There was a slight jolt as the TARDIS landed. The Doctor opened the door and peered out. Sure enough, the TARDIS was back in the quarantine chamber, even standing in exactly the same spot against the wall.

The Doctor beamed, and ushered Sorenson out. 'Come along, Professor, this *is* the Morestran Probe Ship. It's time we rejoined our friends.'

Vishinsky sat in his command chair and studied the rows of instruments in front of him with benign satisfaction. 'We're making good progress now. Once we're across the Galactic Frontier we can signal for an emergency re-fuelling.'

The door slid open and Sorenson and the Doctor entered. 'Doctor,' cried Sarah delightedly.

Vishinsky was staring at the Doctor's companion. 'Professor Sorenson,' he exclaimed. 'Are you all right?'

Sorenson looked baffled and the Doctor said cheerily, 'Don't worry, Vishinsky, the Professor has quite recovered now. In fact he doesn't even remember what's happened. The less said the better, I think.'

'Remember?' said Sorenson indignantly. 'Of course I remember. I've been doing some very important researches. I've discovered a new energy-source, using anti-matter reactions.'

Hurriedly the Doctor said, 'Actually, Professor, I think you'd abandoned that line. Far too many dangers.'

'I had?'

The Doctor took Sorenson to one side. 'You were telling me you'd decided to concentrate on deriving energy from the kinetic force of actual planetary movement,' he said confidentially.

Sorenson was fascinated. 'Was I really?'

'Yes, indeed. In fact you'd worked out some very significant preliminary equations.'

The Doctor snatched a pad from the console, scribbled rapidly and passed it over to Sorenson, who began studying it. 'Yes, of course. The kinetic force of the planets, an immense source of untapped power there. What a brilliant idea!' He frowned, puzzled for a moment. 'I wonder how I came to think of it?'

The Doctor smiled. Strictly speaking he was breaking a Time Lord rule by passing on such information. But it was worth it to divert Sorenson from his disastrous researches into anti-matter. And with all that had happened, the Morestrans were scarcely likely to send another expedition to Zeta Minor.

Sarah was saying good-bye to Vishinsky with real regret. She'd grown very attached to the tough, laconic veteran who had saved their lives. She shook his hand. 'Goodbye, Vishinsky—and thank you!'

Vishinsky began a clumsy speech of thanks, but the Doctor waved it aside. 'My pleasure, old chap, pleased to have been of service. Now, Sarah, we really must be going. We've got an appointment in London and we're already thirty thousand years late.'

A short time later there was a wheezing, groaning noise in the quarantine bay and the TARDIS faded away into the Space/Time Vortex.

So the adventure ended, and they all went their different ways. Sorenson went home to begin the series of brilliant experiments that was to make him the most famous scientist in the Morestran Empire. Vishinsky returned to a hero's welcome, and the promotion that had so long eluded him. And the Doctor and Sarah went off to begin their next adventure.

113322	Barry Letts **DOCTOR WHO AND THE DAEMONS**	(illus)	40p
112873	David Whitaker **DOCTOR WHO AND THE DALEKS**	(illus)	40p
108744	Malcolm Hulke **DOCTOR WHO AND THE DINOSAUR INVASION**		40p
103726	**DOCTOR WHO AND THE DOOMSDAY WEAPON**	(illus)	30p
112601	Terrance Dicks **DOCTOR WHO AND THE GENESIS OF THE DALEKS**		45p
112792	Terrance Dicks **DOCTOR WHO AND THE GIANT ROBOT**		40p
115430	Malcolm Hulke **DOCTOR WHO AND THE GREEN DEATH**	(illus)	40p
108663	Brian Hayles **DOCTOR WHO AND THE ICE WARRIORS**		40p
110412	Terrance Dicks **DOCTOR WHO AND THE LOCH NESS MONSTER**		40p
106555	**DOCTOR WHO AND THE PLANET OF THE SPIDERS**		35p
11308X	Malcolm Hulke **DOCTOR WHO AND THE SEA-DEVILS**	(illus)	40p
1100331	Malcolm Hulke **DOCTOR WHO AND THE SPACE WAR**		45p
110684	Gerry Davis **DOCTOR WHO AND THE TENTH PLANET**		40p
115007	Terrance Dicks **DOCTOR WHO AND THE TERROR OF THE AUTONS**		40p
110846	Terrance Dicks **DOCTOR WHO AND THE WEB OF FEAR**		45p
113241	Bill Strutton **DOCTOR WHO AND THE ZARBI**	(illus)	40p
114477	Terrance Dicks **THE DOCTOR WHO MONSTER BOOK**	(illus)	50p

N.B. 'Doctor Who' Books are published by arrangement with the British Broadcasting Corporation.

Wyndham Books are available from many booksellers and newsagents. If you have any difficulty please send purchase price plus postage on the scale below to:

Wyndham Cash Sales,
123 King Street,
London W6 9JG

While every effort is made to keep prices low, it is sometimes necessary to increase prices at short notice. Wyndham Books reserve the right to show new retail prices on covers which may differ from those advertised in the text or elsewhere.

Postage and Packing Rate

U.K. & Eire
One book 15p plus 7p per copy for each additional book ordered to a maximum charge of 57p.

These charges are subject to Post Office charge fluctuations.